alice on her way

Books by Phyllis Reynolds Naylor

Shiloh Books

Shiloh
Shiloh Season
Saving Shiloh

The Alice Books

Starting with Alice
Alice in Blunderland
Lovingly Alice
The Agony of Alice ◐
Alice in Rapture, Sort of ◐
Reluctantly Alice ◖
All But Alice
Alice in April
Alice In-Between
Alice the Brave ◜
Alice in Lace
Outrageously Alice
Achingly Alice
Alice on the Outside
The Grooming of Alice
Alice Alone
Simply Alice ◖
Patiently Alice
Including Alice

The Bernie Magruder Books

Bernie Magruder and the Case of
    the Big Stink
Bernie Magruder and the
    Disappearing Bodies
Bernie Magruder and the Haunted
    Hotel
Bernie Magruder and the Drive-
    thru Funeral Parlor
Bernie Magruder and the Bus
    Station Blowup

Bernie Magruder and the Pirate's
    Treasure
Bernie Magruder and the Parachute
    Peril
Bernie Magruder and the Bats in
    the Belfry

The Cat Pack Mysteries

The Grand Escape
The Healing of Texas Jake
Carlotta's Kittens
Polo's Mother

The York Trilogy

Shadows on the Wall
Faces in the Water
Footprints at the Window

The Witch Books

Witch's Sister
Witch Water
The Witch Herself
The Witch's Eye
Witch Weed
The Witch Returns

Picture Books

King of the Playground
The Boy with the Helium Head
Old Sadie and the Christmas Bear
Keeping a Christmas Secret
Ducks Disappearing
I Can't Take You Anywhere
Sweet Strawberries
Please DO Feed the Bears

Books for Young Readers

Josie's Troubles
How Lazy Can You Get?
All Because I'm Older
Maudie in the Middle
One of the Third-Grade Thonkers

Books for Middle Readers

Walking Through the Dark
How I Came to Be a Writer
Eddie, Incorporated
The Solomon System
The Keeper
Beetles, Lightly Toasted
The Fear Place
Being Danny's Dog
Danny's Desert Rats
Walker's Crossing

Books for Older Readers

A String of Chances
Night Cry
The Dark of the Tunnel
The Year of the Gopher
Send No Blessings
Ice
Sang Spell
Jade Green
Blizzard's Wake

alice on her way

PHYLLIS REYNOLDS NAYLOR

Atheneum Books for Young Readers
NEW YORK · LONDON · TORONTO · SYDNEY

Atheneum Books for Young Readers
An imprint of Simon & Schuster Children's Publishing Division
1230 Avenue of the Americas
New York, New York 10020

Book design by Ann Zeak
The text for this book is set in Berkley Old Style.
Manufactured in the United States of America
First Edition
2 4 6 8 10 9 7 5 3 1
Library of Congress Cataloging-in-Publication Data
Naylor, Phyllis Reynolds.
Alice on her way / Phyllis Reynolds Naylor.— 1st ed.
p. cm.
Summary: Alice is adjusting to her new stepmother, her brother's
new apartment, her ex-boyfriend, and getting a driver's license.
ISBN 0-689-87090-6
[1. High schools—Fiction. 2. Schools—Fiction.
3. Stepmothers—Fiction. 4. Family life—Fiction.] I. Title.

PZ7.N24Alc 2005
[Fic]—dc22

2004021203

To Sara Cherner, for all her help

Contents

alice on her way

Going Out

My dad's relatives live in Tennessee. Once, on a trip, we stopped in Bristol for lunch. The manager had a clip-on tag with the word *Necessary* on it. Dad smiled at him and said, "I see you're the indispensable one around here."

The manager smiled back and said, "It's my last name. There are lots of us in Bristol."

Lester, my brother, didn't believe him and checked the phone directory on the way out. "There are twenty-seven listed!" he said. "Imagine going through life as Mr. Necessary."

I guess I was thinking about that last Sunday, a January morning so cold that small puddles of icy water collected on the windowsills. Lester came by for brunch, and Dad placed a big dollop of applesauce on each plate beside the pecan pancakes he makes on weekends. It reminded me of the applesauce they served in that restaurant down in Tennessee.

"Mr. Necessary," I said, grinning at Dad. "What would we do without you to make pancakes for us on Sunday mornings?"

Dad smiled. "I guess you'd make them yourselves—no one's indispensable."

"Not even Sylvia?" I asked. My new stepmom was still asleep upstairs. She likes sleeping in on weekends.

The skin at the corners of Dad's eyes crinkled. "Except Sylvia," he said, and smiled some more.

I decided to go for it. "If anything happened to *me*, you'd miss me. Admit it."

Les paused, fork in hand. "Sure we would! I'd say, 'Hey, Dad, you remember that strawberry blonde who used to hang around here—old what's-her-name?'"

I kicked at him under the table and reached for the syrup. I'd sure miss Lester, I know that. I even miss that he doesn't live here anymore, even though he's in an apartment only ten minutes away and drops by a few times a week. Lester moved out because he got this great deal on an apartment he's sharing with two other guys. *He* says he comes by for the pancakes, but *I* think he misses us. We're the only family he has, after all. I'm his only sibling! Don't tell *me* I'm not indispensable!

"Lester," I said, "no matter where you are, you're always part of this family."

"Huh?" said Lester.

"Absence makes the heart grow fonder," I said. "It just makes us appreciate you more when you come over."

"Glad to hear it," said Lester. "You don't really want that second sausage, do you?" He reached over and forked one of them off my plate.

"Go ahead," I told him. "You can be as cool and blasé as you want, but you know how important we are to you."

"Yeah, right!" said Lester.

I got up to read the comics in the living room, and as I left the table he said to Dad, "Now, what did she say her name was again?"

He's impossible! I settled down on the couch with my feet tucked under my robe and thought about the new semester. I was still trying to get used to having my seventh-grade English teacher upstairs in Dad's bed. To Dad and Sylvia's plans to remodel our house. To wearing braces. To not being Patrick's girlfriend anymore. But there were also four big things to look forward to: the Jack of Hearts dance (providing I had a date); a school trip to New York; my sixteenth birthday; and— best of all—my driver's license.

When Lester came through the living room, I said, "You haven't forgotten your promise to teach me to drive, have you?"

"Not when you remind me three or four times a week," he said. "I've got a big paper due the middle of February, though. Wait till the weather's warmer. Then we'll do it."

My brother's in grad school, working on his master's in philosophy. Dad wonders what kind of job he can possibly get with that. Les says he'll sit cross-legged on a mountaintop and people will pay to climb up there and ask him the meaning of life.

"My birthday's in May," I reminded him. "If I'm going to get my license then, I have to take a thirty-hour driver's ed course first. And I don't want to sign up for that until you teach me some of the basics. I don't want to embarrass myself hugely and crash into something."

"Al, if I taught you to drive a Sherman tank and insured you through Lloyd's of London, you'd still probably run into something," Lester said. "Yes, I'll give you some driving lessons, but it won't be in *my* car."

Would it be in Dad's car then? I wondered. He'd traded in his old Honda for a new one—automatic transmission, the works. Could I see him letting me learn to drive in that?

Didn't anyone understand how important this was to me? Being able to drive, to just get in a car and take off, was a basic human need! I *had* to drive! I *needed* to drive! I wanted to transform myself into an exciting new version of me—a woman with car keys in her jeans.

I threw back my head and wailed, "I want to shed this skin and *fly,* Lester!"

"Well, do it in the bathroom, please," Les said.

Of course, I didn't think about driving *all* the time. There were other things on my mind: algebra, our school newspaper, stage crew. A lot of the time I thought about Pamela Jones. Worried about her, you could say.

It's funny about Pamela. Back in sixth grade I used to think she was the girl who had it all. Blond hair so long she could sit on it. She could sing. She could dance. I was jealous as anything. But sometime last year she started losing confidence in herself. She dropped out of Drama Club because she didn't think she was good enough to get a part in the musical. I told her if she didn't sign up for Drama Club this semester, I'd write her name on the sign-up sheet myself, and I did.

It's not like *I* have this great storehouse of self-confidence. I can't even carry a tune. I'm a B student, average height and weight, an okay figure—nothing great. But the only way I'm going to find out what to do with my life is to try different things and see what I do best. What I enjoy

the most. So I'm part of the stage crew for high
school productions. I'm a roving reporter for our
newspaper, *The Edge*. I work part-time at my dad's
music store, and I run a couple of times a week—
just put on my sweats and running shoes and use
that time to work things out in my head.

Sam Mayer is one of the student photographers
for our newspaper. I've known him since we were
in Camera Club together back in eighth grade. We
were dissecting frogs once in our life science class,
and on my birthday he gave me a tiny box with a
frog's heart in it and a note that read, *I'd give you
my own, but I need it.*

He's sixteen already so he's got his license, but
he doesn't have a car—shares one with his mom.

We ran into each other in the hall as I left
American History on Tuesday and headed for algebra. "I liked your article, Alice," he told me. Each
person on the newspaper staff had been given the
assignment to do an in-depth feature article to use
in future issues. I'd titled mine "Who Says?" It was
about the sort of mindless things we do—tradi-
tions, maybe—whether we want to or not. Who
says that the guests have to stand when the bride
comes down the aisle, for example? Who says she
has to have a diamond engagement ring? Who says
we have to eat turkey on Thanksgiving or be with
someone special on New Year's Eve? Who says?

"Thanks," I said. "I've had a lot of good feed-back on it. The last I heard, you were going to write a story on how it feels to break up."

"Dumb idea," Sam said. "Everybody would know I was talking about Jennifer and me. I've decided to do a three-part photo-essay: Where we go when we're not in school, what we do to earn money, and what we give back to the community."

"Sounds good," I told him.

"I'm working on the first part now—where we go outside of school—and thought I'd head for the mall this weekend, take some pictures, ask a few questions. . . . I could use a helper, though. Wanna come?"

"Sure, why not? When?" I said.

"Saturday?"

"Can't. I work for Dad on Saturdays."

"Friday night, then?"

"Okay," I said.

"I heard you're going out with Sam Mayer on Friday," Elizabeth said to me in the cafeteria.

I stared. "I'm just helping him with a piece he's doing for *The Edge*. He only asked me forty minutes ago! How did you know?"

"I heard him telling Patrick."

"*Patrick?*" I said. "Why?"

"I guess Patrick and some of the guys from band

are playing for a faculty dinner Friday night. Patrick asked Sam if the newspaper was going to cover it."

"And . . . ?"

"And Sam said he didn't know, but they'd have to get another photographer because he was going to the mall with you."

Was I glad that Patrick would think I was going out with Sam now? I wondered. Probably.

"Well, Patrick had his chance," said Pamela. "All he thinks about anymore are books."

"Band and books," said Elizabeth.

"Band and books and track," I added.

Elizabeth Price is one of the most beautiful girls in school, but she doesn't know it. She could be chosen Miss America and she still wouldn't believe it. She's got long dark hair and eyelashes to match. Of the four of us—Elizabeth, Pamela, Gwen, and me—she's the only one with a boyfriend, a guy she met at camp last summer who lives in Pennsylvania. Gwen met someone too. For a while she was going out with a guy named Joe, but he goes to another school, and finally that just fizzled.

"We're pathetic," said Pamela, reading my thoughts. She was eating a salad with so much dressing that the green part looked like a garnish. "Not one of us has a date for the Jack of Hearts.

We don't even have boyfriends, and Elizabeth's doesn't count because she hardly ever sees Ross."

"We could hang around the Silver Diner and hope somebody picks us up," Gwen joked. She just had her hair done in a circular pattern of corn-rows and looked fabulous. She probably *would* get picked up. "If nobody asks me by the weekend, I'm going to invite a guy from my church."

"I'll probably invite Brian," mused Pamela.

"Brian?" I said, laughing. "Pamela, I can remember when you said you'd never, ever forgive him because he ruined your wedding night."

Gwen turned. *"What?"*

I saw Elizabeth smiling. She remembered too.

"What did he *do*?" Gwen prodded.

"Put gum in her hair and we couldn't get it out," Liz explained. "She had hair so long, she could sit on it."

"And she was planning to cover her panting, quivering body with her hair like a cape and come to her husband naked on their wedding night," I finished. "We had to take her to a hair salon and have it all cut off. And that's what you see before you today—a short layered look." I grinned.

Pamela was laughing too. "Okay, okay! So I'm going with Brian. Any port in a storm. So I'm des-perate."

"DES-PER-ATE GIRLS!" Gwen and Elizabeth

and I chanted together, and we laughed. It had been the title of an article in the newspaper a month before, about the sexual activity of girls between the ages of twelve and sixteen—how we were getting involved in all kinds of sex, some of which our parents had never heard of, the reporter had written.

"Bring on the kangaroos!" I joked.

Everyone had been talking about that story at school. The thing about "in-depth" articles is that we all know somebody who fits the description, but it never seems to be about us.

"I tore it out of the paper before my dad had a chance to see it," said Pamela. "He already expects the worst."

I didn't know whether my dad had read it or not.

"*My* folks asked me about it," said Elizabeth. "I think they were fascinated by the purity rings."

"Purity rings?" asked Gwen. "I didn't read that part."

"The reporter visited a church where there was a banquet for seventh- and eighth-grade girls and their dads. The fathers all gave their daughters 'purity rings' to wear on the smallest fingers of their left hands as a promise that they were going to stay virgins until they married," Liz explained.

"You're kidding?" said Gwen. "And your dad wanted to give you one?"

"Hardly. He said it would be like leading a bear to honey," said Liz.

"What *is* it about boys and virgins, anyway?" I asked.

"Everyone wants to be the first," said Gwen. "Everyone's looking for a new experience. Me? I just want to experience New York."

"Me too! I can't wait to get up there, ditch a tour, and do something crazy on our own," said Pamela.

"How easy is that going to be?" I asked.

"I don't know, but we'll find a way. And we're all four sharing a room, remember."

"It'll be fun!" said Gwen. "Lights! Broadway!"

"Prada, Fendi!" said Liz.

"Taxis, carriage rides!" I said.

"And guys!" said Pamela.

Sam said he'd be over at seven on Friday.

"New guy?" Sylvia asked me at dinner when I said I was going out. She was wearing black pants, a coral turtleneck, and big fluffy slippers on her feet. We're always teasing Sylvia about the way her feet get cold.

"Just a school buddy," I said.

"Where does he live?" asked Dad.

Great! I thought. *The third degree!* "What does it matter where he lives?" I said. "I'm just helping him with an assignment."

"Well, in case you don't come home, I need to know where to call," said Dad.

I sighed. "His last name is Mayer—M-A-Y-E-R. He lives with his mom in a condo on Colesville Road. I don't know his address. I think she works for the *Gazette.*"

"Well, I want you home by eleven," Dad said. "If you see you're not going to make it, call."

"We'll be back waaaaay before then," I told him.

"Take your cell phone," said Dad.

It's amazing the peace of mind that parents get from a cell phone. I love knowing I can call anybody, anywhere, anytime, but for a parent, it's an umbilical cord. Elizabeth's folks feel the same way.

There wasn't any snow, but it was windy and cold—a biting, wet sort of cold that made you suck in your breath when you stepped outside. Sam got brownie points for coming to the door and ringing the bell.

He's shorter and heavier than Patrick—but still an inch or two taller than I am. Dark hair. His face isn't as round as it used to be, and he's a little more muscular. Has a great smile. Nice eyes. I guess you could say he has that "nice guy" look.

"Digital?" Dad asked him, nodding toward Sam's camera after I'd introduced them.

"It's the only kind we can use for the news-

paper," Sam said. "Everything goes electroni-
cally now."

We said good-bye to Dad and Sylvia, then made
a dash for Sam's car. It was a relief to pull the door
closed after me.

"You look great," Sam told me.

I was in my jacket and gloves and a long angora
scarf that practically reached my ankles. "How can
you tell?" I said, my collar turned up. "All you can
see are my eyes."

"Well, your eyes look great!" he said.

It was the first time I'd been alone with Sam
Mayer. I mean, *really* alone, where nobody could
walk in on us, not that I cared. He had a real mellow CD in the player, and if I wasn't mistaken, I
got a whiff, just a whiff, of a Ralph Lauren cologne.
I know, because Les used to wear it. Sam put on
cologne for *me*?

I glanced sideways at him. He looked like he
always did. *Get real,* I told myself. *This is only an
assignment!*

"So what do you want me to do? How can I
help?" I asked as we turned onto Viers Mill, heading for Wheaton.

"Just keep track of the number of shoots, the
names of the people and their answers," Sam said.
"There's a notebook and pen in my camera bag."

"That's all?"

"People will be more approachable if I have a partner," he said. "I mean, anybody can walk up to a girl, say he's a reporter, and ask if he can take her picture, right? Having you along sort of makes it legit."

"So I'm basically a prop," I said.

"A prop with personality," said Sam, and the music played on.

When we got to Wheaton Plaza and went up the escalator, the first person we ran into was . . . Patrick.

2

"Getting to Know You . . ."

My first thought was that Patrick had come to the mall to check on Sam and me. Maybe I'd wanted him to.

My second thought—the right one—was that he was in a hurry. He was carrying a bag from Hecht's.

"Hey!" he said when he saw us.

"Hey!" I said back.

He paused for a minute, taking us both in— Sam's camera, the notepad in my hand. "How's it going?"

"Haven't started yet. Want to be the first?" said Sam.

"Can't. Dad's waiting for me in the parking lot. I had to buy a dress shirt for tonight." He waved the hand with the bag in it and headed for the down escalator. So much for tender concern.

Sam, though, was studying my face. Both of us

had exes, and I knew what was going through his head. Then he turned and looked around. "What do you think?" he said. "Those guys over there?"

Three boys, probably juniors, were leaning their arms on the railing overlooking the floor below.

"Why not?" I said, and we walked over.

"Hi," Sam said. "I'm doing a photo piece for our school paper and just wanted to ask you a couple questions."

"Yeah?" said the middle guy, turning his head but otherwise not moving an inch.

"What's the question?" another asked.

"Is this where you hang out most when you're not in school?" I said, reading the first of Sam's questions at the top of the page he'd given me.

"This and the Silver Diner," the third one said.

"Okay. Do you come mostly to shop, to meet someone, or just to chill out?" I continued.

The guys looked at each other and grinned. "Chill out *and* meet someone," the first guy said. "Hopefully," he added, grinning.

I got their names and Sam took their picture. We thanked them and moved on.

"It's not very profound," said Sam.

"No, but it has possibilities," I told him.

We found two girls next, coming out of The Limited, each carrying a shopping bag. They giggled when they saw us approaching.

"Care if we take your picture and ask a question?" Sam said. "It's for our school newspaper."

"Depends," said one of the girls. "What do you want to know?" More giggles.

I asked the question. They looked at each other. A group answer seemed to be the norm.

"We always come here," the taller girl said. "I'm returning a Christmas present."

"We shop," said the other. "But we wouldn't mind if we met somebody."

I wondered later if we should tell them about the three guys hanging out by the escalator, but Sam said no.

We did about six or seven interviews, then Sam said we had enough. They were only giving him space for five in the newspaper.

"That wasn't too hard," I said.

"Well, no reason we can't string the evening out a little. Want a latte?" Sam asked.

"That would be good. Make mine mocha," I said, and we went to Starbucks and got a table by the window.

"So when I do my essay on jobs, can I get a picture of you in your dad's store?" Sam asked, putting a mug with a tower of whipped cream in front of me.

"What's to tell?" I asked.

"I'll probably ask (a) how you got the job; (b)

how much you make; and (c) how many hours a week you work."

"Easy," I said. "(a) nepotism—my dad's the manager; (b) minimum wage; (c) Saturdays and sometimes holidays."

"I work for my mom," Sam said. "I bill clients, help her organize her photos, stuff like that. She's freelance but does a lot of work for the weeklies."

"She's a photographer too, right?" I asked.

"Yeah." Sam smiled, and I could tell he was pleased that I'd said "too." He glanced at his watch. "Listen, *The Silent Dark* starts in fifteen minutes. Have you seen it?"

"No. I've heard it's good, though."

"Want to go?"

"If you'll let me buy my own ticket. You paid for the mocha."

"If it'll make you happy," he said.

We walked to the other end of the plaza, and I wondered if we'd get in because of the line. But we managed to get two seats next to the wall in the very last row. I was glad Sam didn't bother with popcorn and drinks, because I like to concentrate on the movie.

The theater was chilly. I was still carrying my jacket and spread it over the front of me like a blanket, pulling it up under my chin. The spooky music didn't help.

"Cold?" Sam whispered.

"A little. It's the music; I'm scared already," I whispered back.

He laughed and put his arm around me, pulling me closer.

The only guy I'd ever been close to like that— besides my dad and Lester, I mean—was Patrick, and it felt strange to be leaning against someone else's shoulder. A broader, better-padded shoulder than Patrick's. Sam's scent, the feel of his jacket, the warmth of his hand on my upper arm . . .

I straightened up when the dialogue began, moving away from him slightly, but he still kept his arm around me.

It was one of those psychological thrillers, where the fear doesn't come from a guy with a chain saw, but from the twists and turns of a woman's mind—that, and her way with rope. First you think that she's sane, and then you think she's not. The horror creeps up on you and you can't escape.

I leaned closer to Sam and heard him chuckle. He took my scarf from my lap and held it against my cheek. "Want your blankie?" he whispered, and made me laugh.

It was a relief when the lights came on at last, even though the madwoman lay dead at the bottom of a ravine.

"Did she jump or did she slip?" I asked Sam as people around us began to gather up their things and leave. It was one of those movies where you weren't sure.

"Slipped," said Sam.

"How do you know? I'd hate for her to have slipped if she really wanted to live."

"Okay, she jumped."

"No." I laughed. "What do you think really happened?"

"I don't know. What do you *want* to have happened?"

I thrust my arms in my jacket sleeves. "You can't just change reality to suit me!" I said. "I want to know what really happened!"

"Slipped," said Sam.

"Jumped!" I told him, and felt him lean forward and kiss the back of my head as we moved out into the aisle.

When we got out to the lobby, I went to the restroom. I was surprised when I looked in the mirror at how red my cheeks were. Flushed. Excited. I rinsed out my mouth and popped a LifeSaver, realizing that I felt a lot different now than I had at the beginning of the evening. We'd started out as school buddies and ended up . . . what? I wasn't sure, but I'd liked leaning against his shoulder in the theater. I liked the way his hand squeezed my upper arm, and I especially liked his kissing the back of my head when we were leaving.

"Oh, wow!" I said when I went back out in the lobby. "It's eleven fifteen. I've got to call Dad." I reached for my cell phone, but Sam offered me his.

"Here," he said. "I just called Mom."

I punched in the number, and Dad answered after the first ring.

"I'm sorry I'm late calling," I said. "We went to a movie after we finished, and it just let out. We're leaving right now."

"Okay, Al. Sylvia and I are going on to bed, and I'll trust you to come straight home," he said.

Sam and I didn't say too much on the way back. He played the rest of the CD. In the headlight beams, I could see a light misty sort of snow coming at us, hitting the windshield and dissolving. The wipers swished occasionally on low speed, and once, where traffic was light, Sam reached over and covered my hand with his, then put it back on the steering wheel.

When we got to my house and parked in the driveway, he reached over and teasingly wrapped my long scarf around and around my neck, then my head, until it felt like a beehive.

"Ready?" he asked, one hand on his door handle.

"Ready," I answered.

We both jumped out at the same time, the wind almost knocking us down, and ran up onto the shelter of the porch. And then, when I tugged the scarf away from my face to tell him good night, he just pulled me to him, like he was keeping me warm, and we kissed. We didn't hurry, I wasn't embarrassed, and my braces didn't matter. The dark helped. The cold helped. The softness of his jacket helped.

"Thanks for coming, Alice," he said.

"It was fun," I told him.

I could see him smiling at me in the dark. And then we kissed again.

I went softly upstairs so as not to wake Dad or Sylvia. I heard Dad cough, though, and knew he probably hadn't let himself sleep till he knew I was safely home. I was smiling, and my cheeks felt even redder than they'd been before. I sat down on my bed in the dark. I just wanted to think about the evening, relive every minute.

Were we "Sam and Alice" now? Were we an "item"?

I looked out the window toward Elizabeth's. She lives in the big white house across the street. A light was on in her bedroom, but I was afraid I'd wake her folks if I called. I took a chance and IM'd her instead. She was online!

AliceBug322: hi
Lovliz13: alice? u just get home?
AliceBug322: yes

Another box popped up—an invitation to Elizabeth's chat room. I clicked OK. Pamela was there too.

Lovliz13: alice just got home
pjhotbabe: so?????
AliceBug322: i had a great time
pjhotbabe: and . . . ????
AliceBug322: he kissed me
Lovliz13: WHAT??????
AliceBug322: 3 times
pjhotbabe: u go, girl!
AliceBug322: one on the back of the head
pjhotbabe: that 1 doesn't count
Lovliz13: if they were lying down it does
AliceBug322: what?
pjhotbabe: were u lying down?
AliceBug322: of course not. he's really nice. we saw The Silent Dark. scary as anything and he had his arm around me the whole time
pjhotbabe: that's how it all begins!!!!!!
AliceBug322: no i mean . . . he's . . . gentle, you know? and funny

pjhotbabe: uh-huh

Lovliz13: i wonder what happened between him and jennifer. i heard she dumped him

pjhotbabe: yeah, i heard it was sort of weird, but then jen's known to be weird sometimes too

AliceBug322: well i've known him since 8th grade and i think he's nice. of course, we never went out or anything. there was always patrick

pjhotbabe: well now's your chance, alice. live a little! patrick's not the only guy who can kiss, you know. so what was it like?

AliceBug322: sweet

pjhotbabe: ugh

AliceBug322: tender, exciting, spontaneous

pjhotbabe: keep going . . .

Lovliz13: did u say anything?

AliceBug322: not while we were kissing!

I told them all about interviewing kids at the mall and the mocha latte and how we saw Patrick. . . .

AliceBug322: i'd better get 2 bed. i've got 2 work tomorrow

Lovliz13: happy dreams! i wish it had
been ross and me
pjhotbabe: passionate dreams! red-hot
sizzling wet drippy heart-palpitating
dreams
Lovliz13: pamela, u r disgusting
AliceBug322: g'nite

I did dream of Sam, but it was all mixed up with
the movie. I think Patrick was even in it somewhere.

"Al," I heard Dad saying at my bedroom door.
"You want to ride in with me, or are you taking the
bus?"

I couldn't believe it was morning already. I
didn't want to wake up. I didn't want to stand out
in the cold waiting for a bus, but if I rode in with
Dad, I had to go early. I let out my breath, then
slowly sat up, swung my legs over the side of the
bed, and tried to keep my eyes open.

"I'll ride with you," I said. The floor was cold,
but I teetered into the bathroom, feeling heavy
and sticky, and realized I'd started my period. My
abdomen always feels fat the first couple of days,
and after I'd washed up and brushed my teeth, I
put on a loose pair of jeans I keep for days like this,
a big baggy sweater, and both a pad and a tampon,
just in case.

Sylvia was still asleep, and Dad had the newspaper spread out on the kitchen table. He glanced up when I came in. "How did it go last night?"

"Okay," I said, and groggily reached for the cereal. "We did five or six shoots, and then we went to the movie. Really scary."

"Is Sam a careful driver?"

"Yes. A slow driver."

"Good," said Dad.

I put an English muffin in the toaster and poured some orange juice. Dad looked over at me again. "You're smiling," he said.

"I am?" I wondered if I'd been smiling all night.

"Sure looks like a smile to me. You had a good time, I take it?" His eyes were laughing.

"Yes. He's nice."

"Uh-huh." Dad waited.

I shrugged. "That's all. I just like him."

"Then I'll need to get used to seeing him around and hope I don't slip up and call him Patrick," said Dad.

"So do I," I said.

3

Alice Blue Gown

I felt like I was smiling at everyone when the Melody Inn opened that morning—customers, employees, the instructors who gave music lessons in the tiny practice rooms on the second floor. We had moved to Maryland from Chicago the summer after second grade, when Dad became manager of a store in Silver Spring. I *think* it was second grade. . . . Mom died when I was in kindergarten. Or was I four . . . ? Have I forgotten dates as important as these, I wonder, or do I repress the sad and scary things in my life? I sure wasn't feeling sad or scared on this particular morning, and Sam was part of the reason.

"Well!" said Marilyn Rawley, Dad's assistant manager. "You're in a happy daze!" She took off her red winter coat and shook the snow out of her hair.

I grinned. "I went out with a new guy," I said.

"Aha!" She darted into the stockroom to hang up her coat, then popped back out again. "Tell all!" she said, eyes all sparkly.

"One of the student photographers on our paper. Sam Mayer. Really funny and kind and muscular. . . . Takes great photos too."

"Ooooh! My kind of guy!" said Marilyn.

I thought about that. Marilyn used to be Lester's number one girlfriend. Well, when he wasn't dating Crystal Harkins, that is. I liked Crystal and Marilyn both. Marilyn was sort of a poster girl for hippies everywhere back then. Long straight hair, cotton dresses, bare feet in summer . . . She played the guitar and sang folk songs. I used to imagine her and Lester getting married in a meadow with a garland of daisies around her head.

Crystal Harkins was just the opposite. Short red hair, elegant, liked classical music . . . If *she* and Lester married, I'd always figured, it would be in a cathedral with a choir of sixty voices singing Bach.

But Crystal married someone else, not too happily, I think, and Marilyn was engaged now. Lester had let two of his favorite girlfriends slip through his fingers because he wasn't ready.

When I'd finished telling Marilyn about my evening with Sam, I said, "What about *you*? When are you and Jack getting married?"

"In June," she said, and her voice practically bubbled, she was so eager to tell me. "And you're all invited."

All? I wondered. "You're sending Les an invitation too?" I asked.

"We're not sending out invitations. I'm telling people in person," Marilyn said. "It's just a simple ceremony, Alice, the kind I've always wanted. It's going to be outdoors at a nature center and—"

"I *knew* it!" I shrieked. "I *knew* that's the kind of wedding you'd have."

David, our newest employee—a young good-looking guy who's thinking of becoming a priest—came in just then.

"What's this? Am I invited too?" he teased.

"All my nearest and dearest," Marilyn said. "Of course you are."

"And if it rains?" I asked her.

"Then we'll bring umbrellas," said Marilyn, and I believed her.

What I like about Marilyn is that she doesn't have any of that "princess syndrome," that "*my* day" attitude, as though you become royalty on your wedding day and everyone has to obey you. I've heard of brides who spaz out because someone coughed during the ceremony. Marilyn wouldn't let even a thunderstorm upset her.

I'm sort of on call at the store to do whatever

needs doing—wash a window, dust a countertop, stock shelves—but mostly I'm in charge of the Gift Shoppe on Saturdays, the little alcove under the stairs to the second floor. We sell all kinds of musical gifts. I bought a sterling silver clef sign pin for Sylvia once, back when I was campaigning to make her my stepmom.

When Dad came by on his way down from the second floor, I said, "Did you know that Marilyn and Jack are getting married in June and we're invited?"

I guess he already knew. "We'll be there," he said, "with or without umbrellas."

What surprised me was that Sam called me at work. That's a real no-no. You just don't call people at work; you might get them fired.

"Pretend I'm a customer," he said, and I could almost see the smile in his voice. "I just wanted to tell you that I enjoyed last night. Especially the end of the evening."

How was I supposed to pretend I was listening to a customer? I could feel the blush in my cheeks.

"So did I," I murmured softly, covering the mouthpiece with my hand.

Dad gave me a look, and I told Sam I'd talk to him later. It was a serious, quizzical kind of look I hadn't seen on his face before. I'm sure he knew it wasn't a customer.

"Okay," I told Dad before he could say a word, "I'll tell him not to call here again."

On the way home that night with Dad, I said, "Is Marilyn going to work for you after she's married?"

"She says she is. I'd hate to lose her. Marilyn knows music from A to Z—folk, classical, rock, jazz. And the customers love her," Dad said.

I sighed. "So do I. So did Lester." I stared out the window awhile, then said, "Do you think he'll turn out to be a lonely old bachelor because he can't commit?"

I couldn't tell if Dad was choking or laughing. "A *lonely* old bachelor? *Lester*? Al, he's only twenty-three. If he doesn't 'commit' for the next ten years, it'll be all right with me!"

I think Sylvia likes having the house to herself on Saturdays. With Dad and me gone all day, she spreads her coursework out over the dining-room table and uses the time to grade papers and prepare tests and stuff.

But by the time we're home, she has the table in the kitchen set and dinner in the oven. This night it was salmon with dill sauce and rice with slivers of almonds in it. There was even a loaf of home-made bread.

I told her about Marilyn getting married in a

meadow, just as I had predicted. "It wouldn't surprise me if she's barefoot too," I said.

Sylvia laughed. "It wouldn't surprise me if every bride *wished* she were barefoot by the time she gets to the reception. Those satin heels really do a number on your feet."

We dug into the salmon then, and the table talk turned mundane. I used to fantasize that when Dad and Sylvia were married, we would have exciting, stimulating conversations at the dinner table, about travel in Rome and Shakespeare's sonnets. But now they were talking "house."

"The more I think about it," said Dad, "I wonder if we shouldn't put off the renovation till next year. Replace the furnace and air conditioner first. Get this part of the house in shape before we do an addition."

Sylvia toyed with her rice. "I hate to put it off, but I think you're right. And we might want to consider double-pane windows while we're at it. That would give us a little more time to go over the design and make sure we've got all the things we want in a master bedroom."

I yawned. With Valentine's Day coming up, I'd have thought they'd be discussing a trip to Paris or something, not double-pane windows. But, like the saying goes, whatever turns you on. . . .

• • •

You know what's weird? Going to school for the first time after you've kissed a guy and facing him again in daylight.

I mean, kissing in the dark has its advantages— you can't really see each other's expressions. In the cold, in the wind, and snuggled up against his jacket, almost anything you'd say might sound romantic. How would I feel when I met up with him in the hall, surrounded by metal lockers and kids laughing and milling around? It wouldn't seem very romantic then. Would Friday night seem silly now? Phony?

I hung up my jacket and got out my science book. I'd just started down the hall when I felt an arm around my waist.

"How you doing?" Sam said, his mouth next to my ear. I startled, then smiled.

"Oh! Hi," I said, trying desperately to remember if I'd brushed my teeth after breakfast or if this had been one of those mornings I'd made a dash for the bus stop. I hate it when I find bread stuck in my braces. I ran my tongue along my top teeth.

"I wanted to catch you this morning before anyone else did," Sam said, moving along the hallway beside me. "I'd like to take you to the Jack of Hearts."

Wow! I thought. There are four major dances at our school: the Homecoming Dance in October, casual, at our school; the Snow Ball in early December, formal; the Jack of Hearts dance around Valentine's Day, semi-formal; and the Senior Prom.

Back in junior high we had an eighth-grade semi-formal, and Sam had asked me first. But I'd told him I was "sort of going with Patrick Long," which I was, except he hadn't asked me to the dance yet. When Patrick found out I was upset he hadn't asked me—just *assumed* we'd be going—he'd got down on one knee on the bus and asked me to go, and everyone laughed. That made it all right. But now it was three weeks before Valentine's Day, and if Patrick was still interested in me, which I thought maybe he was, the way we had danced at Dad and Sylvia's wedding, he hadn't asked me.

"Sure," I said to Sam. "I'd love to go."

"Oh . . . my . . . God!" Elizabeth said in the cafeteria when I told the other girls. We were all sitting at one table, and the guys were sitting at the one next to ours, discussing the Super Bowl. All but Patrick and Sam, who had a different lunch period this semester.

The topic of conversation at our table was the Jack of Hearts.

"Hey!" said Pamela when she heard the news. "That was fast!"

"He doesn't waste any time, that boy," said Gwen. She and her friend Yolanda had asked two boys from their church. Pamela was going to the dance with Brian, Penny was going with Mark Stedmeister, Karen hadn't been asked yet, and Jill, of course, was going with Justin.

If anybody fits that newspaper article's profile about girls and sex, it's Jill, because she's always talking about it. Sex, that is. I don't see her as exactly desperate, though. She just wants us all to know that she and Justin are hot and heavy.

It begins to get to me after a while. I get the feeling she wants us to ask her about it just so she can brag. Like, we'll be talking about something entirely different. Someone might say, "He's the top man on the team," and Jill will smile and say, "Well, *some*times the woman's on top." Stupid stuff like that, like she's trying to turn everything around to her and sex.

"I wish I could get Ross to come down for the dance," said Elizabeth wistfully.

"Did you ask him? Maybe he will," I said.

"He doesn't have his license yet. His brother would have to drive him all the way from Philadelphia, and then where would they stay? I mean, it turns into a really big deal."

"Maybe they could stay at Lester's apartment," I suggested.

"Really?" Elizabeth looked thoughtful. "I don't know, but I'll ask Ross and see what he says."

"Who do you suppose Patrick is taking?" asked Pamela.

"Who knows?" I said. And added, "Who cares?" except I wasn't sure I meant it. Patrick *was* busy, I knew that. Too busy to bother with school dances, probably. Anyone who signs up for an accelerated program—getting through high school in three years instead of four—has got to use every spare minute he has. But even if he *was* interested in me again, would I want to take second place to everything else in his life?

We talked then about who had a license and whose parents were available to drive. The Jack of Hearts wasn't the kind of dance you came to in a limo. Guys wore suits or blazers, and girls wore heels and slinky dresses. It took place in our gym, not some hotel.

We set about discussing a date for Karen, and by the time I went to phys ed afterward, we had it all arranged. Later, after I'd showered and went to the mirrors to fix my hair, Jill and Karen and one of the juniors saw me coming. Watching my eyes in the mirror, Jill started to sing and the other girls laughingly joined in. It was a parody of an old song with my name in it, "Alice Blue Gown."

In fact, Jill wouldn't know this, but it was the

song Uncle Milt used to sing to me when I was little. Aunt Sally took care of us for a while after Mom died, and after I'd had my bath at night and had put on my nightgown, I'd crawl up on Uncle Milt's lap and he'd read me a story. And then he'd sing:

> "In my sweet little Alice blue gown,
> When I first wandered down into town,
> I was both proud and shy, as I felt every eye,
> But in every shop window I'd primp passing by;
> Then in manner of fashion I'd frown,
> As the world seemed to smile all around,
> Till it wilted I wore it, I'll always adore it,
> My sweet little Alice blue gown."

I'd always loved that song. I liked the way Uncle Milt sang it to me. But now Jill and Karen and the other girl were belting out a risque version they must have learned after lights-out at camp somewhere:

> "In my sweet little nightie of blue,
> On the night that I first slept with you,
> I was both shy and scared, as the bed was prepared,
> For I knew what my mother had told me was true.

It is now several months since that night,
And my nightie has grown very tight.
You thrilled me, you chilled me, you gosh-
darn near killed me,
In my sweet little nightie of blue."

Pamela, at the opposite row of mirrors, laughed and so did I as I squeezed in between her and Elizabeth, but I could feel my cheeks burning. I *hate* that my cheeks give me away. It wasn't the song that was embarrassing but the fact that I felt Jill had sung it just for me, because of my name. Because she always treats me as such an innocent.

As we were leaving the locker room Elizabeth said to me, "It's stuff like that that makes virgins scared."

"Huh?" I said.

"That line, 'You gosh-darn near killed me.'"

"Rhymes with 'chilled,'" I told her.

"It's another way of saying she almost died of pleasure," said Pamela. "Thrilled, chilled, had her socks knocked off . . ."

"Not necessarily," said a voice behind us, and it was the third girl who'd been singing with Karen and Jill. "Just between you and me, I don't know a single girl who enjoyed her first time." Then she gave us a bemused smile and walked on.

It seemed to me then that there was a whole lot

more sex going on than I knew about, or maybe people just lie, I don't know. Maybe that newspaper article was true! But why is it, I wondered, that no matter what I do, I sort of feel like whatever the mainstream is doing, I'm not with it. That a party's going on and I'm not invited. That everyone else has this wonderful, exotic, erotic life . . .

It would be nice to surprise everybody and do something wild for a change, I thought, but I didn't know exactly what that would be.

4

Plans

Our school puts on a major production each spring. One year it's the senior play, the next year it's either an operetta or a musical. If it's a play, only the seniors get parts. But if it's a musical where a large cast is required and they all have to sing, anyone can try out.

Because it was *Fiddler on the Roof* last year, this year it would be a play. And since Pamela wasn't eligible to be in it, so couldn't be disappointed if she didn't get a part, I decided it was the perfect time to get her back in the Drama Club and working backstage with me. I practically dragged her to our first meeting, the first week of February.

The stage crew meets in a rehearsal room once a week after school, but two weeks or so before the performance we meet every day plus weekends. Often enough to keep Pamela out of trouble, I figured.

Since her parents' marriage went down the tube, Pamela's practically gone down with it. If your mom takes off to be with some boyfriend, how can you help but feel she'd rather be her boyfriend's girlfriend than your mom? And even though you know in your head that the trouble was between her and your dad, how can you stop feeling that you're not a cute enough daughter, or loving enough, or smart enough to keep her home? That maybe she just doesn't care all that much?

It doesn't seem to help that Mrs. Jones is back in the picture now, living in an apartment alone and pestering Pamela with phone calls, wanting to take up where she left off, and thinking everyone will forget what happened. I don't think Pamela or her dad will ever forget. It's as though her friends, not her parents, have become Pamela's family. I'd noticed that Brian, in particular—now that they were going to the dance—was getting his share of affection. Maybe more than his share. Each of them was always a flirty kind of person, but this seemed to be more than the usual kid stuff back in junior high.

Now, sitting around with some of the stage crew at school, legs sprawled out in front of her as though we'd have to use a cattle prod to get her standing again, Pamela said, "So? What are we supposed to do?"

Just at that moment a couple of seniors came in—Harry, from last year, and a blond-haired guy, Chris. As soon as Pamela saw them, she straightened up and kept watching the door to see what the rest of our crew looked like.

I was watching the door for a different reason, though. I'd read the names on the sign-up sheet and knew that Molly, with the huge blue eyes, would be with us again this year. So would Charlene Verona. But the person I was watching for was a senior named Faith, and here she came—rail thin, dressed in the usual black jersey top, long black skirt and granny boots with impossibly pointed toes, black mascara around her eyes. She wore bright red lipstick outlined in black against her pale skin.

We were all glad to see her because she was like a frail sister to us, and we worried about her. Not her health. Her boyfriend.

"Hi, Faith!" I said, grabbing her hand as she passed me and sat down on the other side of Molly. "How *are* you?" What I *really* wanted to say was, *You're not still going out with that scumbag Ron, are you?*

Mr. Ellis came in then and announced that the spring play would be *Father of the Bride*. (The stage crew is always the first to find it out.) The set wouldn't be as elaborate as we'd had last year for

Fiddler, he told us—creating a Russian village—but he wanted to keep the play contemporary, and we'd need to put together a complete living room.

Then he assigned crew managers—Harry, sets; Faith, props; Charlene, costumes; Molly, electrical—and let the rest of us choose what committee we wanted to work on. Pamela chose to work on props with Faith, but I wanted something different this time, so I volunteered to work on sets with Harry.

Through it all, I kept watching the door and could see that Molly was too. Last year Ron had sat in on some of our meetings and was totally obnoxious when it came to Faith—the way he'd order her around, push her, insult her. When the meeting was over and he still hadn't come in, we began to hope that we'd talked some sense into Faith about dropping him. Then we went out into the hall and saw him leaning against a locker, waiting for her. She went over and kissed him, and he guided her on toward the door, one hand on the back of her neck.

Molly sighed. "Maybe he's changed," she said hopefully.

"Yeah, and maybe the pope's Protestant," I said.

"What's the matter with him?" Pamela wanted to know.

"Control freak," said Molly. "First-class, grade-A, the genuine article."

"And Faith puts up with it?" asked Pamela.

"All the way," I said.

I think that orthodontists do their training on torture equipment. First they learn how to crunch your lips between your teeth and their fist, and then they work on tightening the wires. I was thinking about this as I sat gripping the armrests of Dr. Wiley's padded torture chair. I mean, what kind of person decides to make tightening wires around teeth his life's work? Doesn't that make you wonder?

Dr. Wiley paused to get something out of a cupboard and caught me studying his certificates and diplomas on the wall. *Glowering* at them, actually.

"Problem?" he asked.

"Yeah," I said. "I wondered what Marine boot camp you trained in." That was rude, I know, but I was feeling rude. He hurts me, I hurt him.

At first he was taken aback a little. Then he said, "I try to be as gentle as I can, but some of the pain is unavoidable. I'm sorry." And then he added, as though he could read my thoughts, "Why don't we focus on the end result—straight teeth and a healthy mouth. That's what gives me satisfaction."

Touché. I don't want to enter the medical profession, but if I did, I'd be an obstetrician. When you think about it, obstetricians are the only doctors who are called on to treat a happy, natural condition. Everything else is a sickness.

"Your teeth are doing fine, by the way," the orthodontist told me.

"Any chance the braces can come off early?" I asked.

"We'll wait and see about that," he said.

I was surprised when I left the office and entered the lobby to see Sam sitting on a bench waiting for me.

"What are *you* doing here?" I asked, my mouth sore. I could feel a headache coming on too.

He grinned and stood up. "I called your house, and your stepmom told me where you were. I just thought you might like to have a ride home."

I would. I just didn't feel like talking a lot. All I wanted to do was curl up on my bed and listen to music and be grumpy. But it was nice of him to come for me.

As we turned off Wayne Avenue, Sam said, "We've got an invitation. Mom wants to have a little dinner for us before the dance. You know, restaurant style, but at our place."

"Your mom?" I said. She didn't even know me.

"Yeah. She likes to do stuff like that."

"Who all will be there?"

"You and me and anyone else we want to invite."

"Well, okay," I said.

We drove a little farther, and Sam glanced over at me. "You look like you have a headache."

"I do, actually. I'm not very good company after I see the orthodontist," I said.

He reached over and squeezed my hand. "You don't have to say anything."

Would Patrick have come to pick me up after a dental visit? I wondered. I didn't know, but I was glad to get home and glad that Sam didn't ask to come in.

"Thanks," I told him, and when he leaned over and gave me a kiss, he said, "You even smell like the orthodontist," and we laughed.

I'd barely stepped inside the house when Elizabeth called.

"He's coming!" she said.

"Who?"

"Ross! To the dance!"

"Oh, Liz, that's great!"

"He's coming down on the train, so his brother won't have to drive him. Mom says she'll be more comfortable if he stays at Lester's, but if that doesn't work out, he can stay with us."

"I'll ask," I promised. "And listen. Sam's mother is giving a dinner for us in their condo before the dance. You and Ross want to come?"

"In their condo?"

"Yeah. She likes to . . . you know . . . make like a restaurant, Sam says. Then you won't have to worry about where to take Ross before the dance."

"Okay. Sure!" said Liz.

I was about to phone Lester when he walked in the door. He and his two roommates live in a second-floor apartment in a big Victorian house in Takoma Park. They get it rent-free from an elderly man named Otto Watts, who lives downstairs, with the understanding that one of them will always be there at night in case Otto needs him. They pay their own utilities and do odd jobs around the place.

"I smell lasagna," he said, hanging up his jacket. Sylvia must have invited him for dinner.

"Hi, Les," she called from the kitchen. "It's spaghetti, actually."

She always fixes something soft and easy to chew on days I get my braces tightened. That's the kind of things moms do, I guess. I watched Lester pick up a magazine and slouch down on the couch. He seemed relaxed and in a good mood, but I knew I couldn't just spring something on him. So I said, "Lester, if you could do a favor for a friend of mine that would mean everything in the world to her, would—?"

"No," said Lester, without looking up.

"You don't even know what I'm going to ask. Next to the prom, it's the most important dance of the year, and—"

"I am not taking Pamela to the dance, no matter how sad, lonely, miserable, misunderstood—"

"I'm not talking about Pamela."

"*Elizabeth's* miserable and misunderstood?"

"No. It's about sleeping over at your apartment."

"Are you crazy?"

"Not Elizabeth! Her date!"

"Al, start at the beginning," he said.

"I'm *trying*! Liz met this great guy at camp. He lives in Philadelphia, but he's going to come down on the train and be her date for the Valentine's dance. Her mom said they'd be more comfortable if he didn't stay there, and I wondered if he could possibly spend the night at your place when he comes."

Lester looked at me over the top of the magazine. "Somebody else picks him up at Amtrak and brings him to the apartment?"

"Right."

"Somebody else picks him up for the dance and brings him back afterward?"

"Right."

"And somebody else sees that he gets to the train on time the next day?"

"Right again. All you have to do is let him sleep on your couch."

"Without Elizabeth."

"I promise. You don't have to worry about Elizabeth. She wants to stay a virgin," I said. Then I thought about Ross kissing her naked breasts at camp. "Technically, I mean. Below the waist, anyway."

"I don't think I need to know all that," said Lester. "Tell her it's okay."

"*Thank* you, Lester!" I said, and immediately called Elizabeth to tell her. She said to tell Lester that if she could ever do a favor for him, all he had to do was ask.

"Thanks but no thanks," said Lester. "She's too complicated for me."

5

How *Could* He?

At dinner that night I got a shock. I mentioned that Les was going to let Ross stay at his place the night of the dance, and Sylvia asked if the dance was on a Friday or Saturday night. Dad said he hoped it wasn't a Saturday because there was church the next morning. And then—like, out of the blue—he said, "I've been meaning to tell you, Al, that I sort of went out on a limb here and signed you up for a class at church. I hope you don't mind."

It was so unlike him that I could only stare. *"What?"* I said. "What kind of class?"

"It's called 'Our Whole Lives,' and it's for high school students only."

I tried to take that in. "Whole, meaning . . . ?"

"Intellectual, spiritual, physical," Dad began.

"Sexual," said Lester, and shoved some spaghetti into his mouth.

I exploded. All I could think about was that church function where they handed out purity rings. "You're sending me to church to learn about sex?"

"It's only once a week for a couple of months," Dad said.

"We studied that back in junior high!" I spluttered.

"I know, but this is from a different perspective. I'd really like for you to take it, Al."

I pushed away from the table. "No! What right did you have doing that without even asking me?"

"No right at all, really. But they had an opening and—"

"Why did you *do* this?" I yelled, ignoring the surprise on Sylvia's face. "What got you started on this? It's Sam, isn't it?"

"Of course not. I just heard about it at church, and it sounded good to me."

"Well, it doesn't sound good to me." I looked helplessly about the table, but Sylvia gave me a sort of bemused "Sorry" look, and it was obvious I'd get no help from her. "I'm not going!" I said, standing up and banging my chair against the table. "You didn't show even an ounce of respect for me, Dad, by signing me up like I was five years old. Now you can *un*sign me." I went upstairs and slammed my door. Hard.

I sure didn't need this. My teeth were still hurting from the orthodontist. I'll have to admit, though, that once I was in my room, I was as puzzled as I was angry. *What made him do it?* I kept asking myself. I don't think it was Sylvia's idea. It *had* to be that he was worried about Sam. Maybe he just didn't feel he knew him as well as he'd known Patrick. Maybe it was the way I'd been talking to Sam on the phone when he called the Melody Inn that one time—maybe something about that had set him off.

I was still sitting on the side of my bed hyperventilating when Dad tapped on the door and came in. I glared at him. He pulled out my desk chair and turned it, facing me. "May I?" he asked, sitting down.

"Do I have a choice?" I said.

"I overstepped, Al, and I'm sorry. I didn't ask you first because I was afraid you'd say no."

"You guessed right," I told him. "I hardly know anyone at that church! I've hardly ever gone."

"Well, maybe this is a good time for you to get acquainted, then," Dad said, trying to be cheerful.

"Dad, we were practically raised heathen! I'm not prepared!"

"You were not raised heathen, Al. People can be good without belonging to a church. Those kids aren't any different from you."

"You're worried about Sam and me. Admit it."

"Honey, I'll worry about *all* the boys you'll meet from here on," he said truthfully.

"Why weren't you worried about Patrick?" I demanded, remembering the time in his basement when his mom was out and he was giving me a drum lesson. The way he ran his hands up my sides close to my breasts and I could almost feel myself beginning to melt.

Dad frowned a little. "*Should* I have been?"

"Maybe," I said, just to torment *him* a little. And suddenly I thought I knew. "It was that newspaper article, *wasn't* it? 'Desperate Girls'!"

I saw the color creeping up into my dad's face. He was actually blushing!

"It was! It was!" I crowed.

"Well, it did get my attention," he told me.

I sat studying my father, trying to remember everything that reporter had written. The title, "Desperate Girls," and then the subtitle, "Looking for Thrills, Looking for Acceptance, Looking for Love." "You think that's *me*?"

"No. I hope not, anyway. But listen, Al. You're not going to tell me everything from here on, and I'm not going to ask. I know that. It's normal. But the teen years are hard on parents *because* of that. I promised Marie I'd do the best I could with you. And after I met Sylvia, I promised *myself* I wouldn't dump all the responsibility for raising you on her. I read things. I listen to the people at work talk about problems they have with their kids. I try to keep up with what's going on, and I've heard wonderful things about that class at Cedar Lane."

"*What* things?"

"It's all about communication and respect and intimacy. Younger kids can't even attend." He was trying to appeal to my ego, I could tell.

"How do you know so much about it?" I asked.

"No student can take it unless a parent attends two sessions, so I—"

"You're going to be there *with* me?" I cried.

"No, no. I've already gone to the sessions for parents so I could see what they talk about and what you'd be reading." And then he leaned forward and looked right into my eyes. "I know I went about this all wrong, Al. But I'm asking you to do it for me. Humor an old dad who's been a single parent for much too long."

I don't know if it was because I felt sorry for him right then or because I needed his car to learn to drive in, but I finally—reluctantly, grumpily—said an almost inaudible "Okay."

When I came downstairs later, Dad and Sylvia had gone out, but Les was still hanging around looking for leftovers in the fridge.

"Why didn't Dad make *you* take that class when *you* were in high school?" I grumbled.

"Because I already knew how to put a condom on a banana," said Les.

"I have to put a condom on a banana?" I gasped. "Why do I have to know how to do that?"

"Because a man might want you to do it sometime," said Lester.

I was a "Desperate Girl," all right, but I wasn't looking for thrills or acceptance or love right then; I was looking for a sane human being to talk to. I got on the phone with Elizabeth. "You're not going to believe what Dad's making me do," I said. "He's signed me up for a sex class at church."

"At *church*?" she said. "There's probably nothing to it, then, Alice. You'll just sign a chastity card or something."

"I don't think so," I told her. "We practice putting a condom on a banana."

"What?" she cried. "In front of the congregation?"

Even I had to laugh a little. "Not then. I think Dad's worried about Sam."

"Listen, we haven't done half the things *some* of the sophomores do," Liz said.

"Yeah," I joked. "We've got a lot of catching up to do."

"Well, whatever you learn in that course, teach

me," said Elizabeth. "If you learn it in church, it must be okay."

I was curled up on my bed listening to a CD, waiting for the Tylenol to kick in, when I got a call from Patrick on my cell phone.

"Hey!" he said. "How are ya?"

"Hurting," I said, surprised. "I got my braces tightened this afternoon."

"Oh. Bummer. Bad, huh?"

"The orthodontist graduated from Sadist School."

Patrick laughed. "How much longer does the torture go on?"

"A year more if I'm lucky. A year and a half if I'm not."

"Well, on a brighter note, I wondered if you'd like to go to the Jack of Hearts with me," he said.

I was totally speechless. My first thought was *He still likes me!* My second was *It's February second! The dance is on the eleventh! What is he, Clueless in Silver Spring?*

"You're a little late, Patrick," I said. "I'm going with Sam."

"Oh." Patrick was quiet a moment, then he said, "Did he ask *you* or what?"

Now, *that* made me mad. As though the only way I'd get to a dance was to do the asking. "Yes, he asked!" I told him.

"Well then, I guess the answer's no?" said Patrick.

My jaw dropped and I sat up on one elbow. What did he think? That he could just ask me whenever and I'd drop the other guy like a hot potato and go with him? "Of course it's no!" I said. "I *want* to go with Sam."

"Oh. Well, sure. I guess I don't expect you to back out of it," he said. And then, after another pause, "Maybe I'm just wondering where that leaves me."

Up a creek without a paddle? I wanted to say. Then I realized that maybe he was *afraid* I'd taken the initiative and asked Sam. Maybe he was wondering if I'd chosen Sam instead of him. "Don't worry, Patrick," I said. "There are at least a dozen girls who would give anything to go with you."

"Well, that's good to know. You want to give me a list?" he said.

I laughed. He laughed. A little. "Well, anyway, have a good time at the dance," he said. And hung up.

I couldn't quite get over it, though. He *must* still like me! He'd been thinking about me anyway, and I wondered what he'd been thinking. What he remembered. I wondered if we still remembered the same things.

On the one hand, it was exciting having *two* boys ask me to the dance, but on the other, I wondered why Patrick hadn't asked me sooner. Had his first choice turned him down? And who did I really want to go with, him or Sam?

Partly, though, I was thinking that maybe the reason Patrick hadn't asked me earlier was that he's one of the busiest guys I know. He works hard at everything—school, band, track. . . . Once he entered the accelerated program, he started taking two more courses than the rest of us, and it seems so unnecessary. What's the rush?

And yet I liked the way he seemed to have his life—well, the next few years anyway—all mapped out. He knew what he wanted to do and where he wanted to go. Gwen's the same way. Already she's thinking about where she wants to go to college and where she might get a scholarship. When I listen to her talk sometimes, I panic.

Why don't I know where I want to go to college? Why don't I know exactly what I want to do or be? I can remember when I thought I wanted to be a basketball player or a chef. A veterinarian, even! I like working on the newspaper, though, so maybe I should study journalism. And I like people—I like trying to understand why they do what they do—so maybe I should be a psychologist. Those are the two things that stick with me the most.

"If you go for a psychology degree, you can get

either a bachelor of arts or a bachelor of science," Gwen told me.

"What's the difference?" I asked.

"If you choose the BA degree, you'll study people-oriented stuff, like sociology. If you choose the BS, you'll take a lot more math and science."

"Bachelor of arts!" I croaked. Gwen has a scientific mind, but I don't. I wouldn't even be making it through Algebra II if she weren't helping me. The teacher goes too fast, and I'm too scared to get half of what he says. Sometimes I feel I don't even understand enough to ask an intelligent question.

"I wish I were more like you," I said, staring down at her brown hand with the long, elegant nails. That's another way we're different—Gwen puts a lot of time into her nails. I put a coat of clear polish on mine once a week and call it done. "You know just what you want to do with your life."

"Not!" said Gwen.

"I thought you wanted to major in music and become a singer."

"I don't think so," she said. "I'd only want to do that if I could become another Kathleen Battle or Jessye Norman."

"Who?"

"Concert singers. Classical, spirituals, opera . . . And my chances of that are about one in a million." She shook her head. "If, after all the training, I just ended up directing a local choir, I don't think I could be happy. So now I'm thinking of going into medicine, with music on the side."

I let out my breath and stared at the doodles I'd been making on my work sheet. I'd drawn a large oval at the bottom of the page, a smaller one beside it.

"What are those supposed to be?" asked Gwen.

"Brains," I said. "Yours and mine."

6

Mothers

On the bus the next day Pamela told us she was taking a driver's ed course on Saturdays. We were all trying to fit that thirty-hour course in somewhere. "Do you realize that once we get our licenses, we can drive to school?" she said. "No more getting up early and standing out in the freezing cold."

Elizabeth loosened the scarf around her neck. "Providing one of us gets a car."

"Details, details," said Pamela. "Listen. Mom has been nagging me to come over, and I don't want to go alone. Will you come with me?"

"Why? You spent New Year's Eve with her, didn't you?" asked Liz.

"Yes, but it was a disaster. Now she says she's turned her spare room into *my* room, and I don't want to live with her!"

I didn't want to go, and I don't think Liz did

either. But we both hated to see Pamela holding a grudge for the rest of her life.

"When?" I asked.

"Uh . . . this afternoon, maybe? She says she found a dress for me at Nordstrom to wear to the dance. It's blackmail, of course, because if I want it, I have to come get it."

"What color?"

"Black and red. It sounds good, the way she described it, and she gets an employee's discount. What are you going to wear?"

"Mom and I found a rose crepe dress at Hecht's," Elizabeth said. "Mom's taking up the hem, though, making it shorter. What about you, Alice?"

To tell the truth, I had opened my closet door, rummaged through the hangers, then closed it again. It was just too much to think about. I like having nice clothes, I just hate the trying on and deciding.

"I don't know," I said. "Probably the bridesmaid's dress I wore at Crystal's wedding. It's cocktail length."

Both Pamela and Elizabeth turned and looked at me. "Alice, that was two years ago," said Liz.

"So?" I said.

"So you've *grown*!" said Pamela. "You've got breasts! Have you tried that dress on lately?"

I had a sinking feeling. I remembered that even the backless dress I had worn to Lester's New Year's Eve party had been too tight across the stomach.

"The dress I wore for Dad's wedding, then?" I pleaded.

"With spaghetti straps? Isn't that a little too . . . too . . . cold for February?" said Elizabeth.

"Too summery," said Pamela. "Definitely too summery."

I stared straight ahead. "I'll think of something," I said.

"How do we get to your mother's?" Elizabeth asked Pamela.

"We'll take the city bus straight up Georgia Avenue to the Glenmont Apartments," Pamela told us. "I'll call and tell her we're coming."

It was half raining, half sleeting when we left school that afternoon. We crowded under the Plexiglas shelter at the city bus stop, our hair wet, fingers cold. When the bus came, we trooped to the back and sat together, huddled for warmth, and watched the office buildings give way to apartment complexes as we went north.

"I'm not looking forward to this," Pamela said after a while. "I'm so mixed up about her, I don't know *how* I feel."

"Yeah?" I said.

"I want things back like they used to be, and I know that can't happen. On one hand, I'm worried about her, and on the other, I don't even want to talk to her. That's where you guys come in. If I clam up, *you* do the talking," Pamela said.

"It's *you* she most wants to see, Pam," I said.

"She's the only mom you've got," said Elizabeth.

"Lucky me," said Pamela.

There were several buildings in the Glenmont Apartments complex, and Mrs. Jones was in the second building set back from the street. We got off the bus and slogged our way up the sidewalk, then stomped our feet on the hall carpet when we got inside.

"It's up one flight and to the left," said Pamela.

We knocked, and within seconds, Mrs. Jones answered. I'll bet Pamela didn't tell her that Liz and I were coming along. I wasn't sure if she was glad or disappointed.

"Well, Alice! Elizabeth! What a nice surprise!" she said. "Oh, you girls are soaked. Come in and let me get some towels."

We went inside and slipped off our shoes.

The thing about Mrs. Jones is, she thinks *she's* a teenager. She dresses more like Pamela's sister than her mom—skintight jeans, stretchy tops, chunky or delicate jewelry, whatever's in fashion.

We stood in the hallway in our stocking feet

while she produced towels, and we dried our hair and shook the water off our jackets.

"So . . . this is your apartment!" said Liz.

"Yes! Let me show you around," said Mrs. Jones. "I was really lucky to get this one, because it overlooks the woods back there. I even saw a fox the other day, can you imagine?"

The furniture was sort of retro—art deco style, but she'd mixed in a few things from Crate and Barrel, and it worked. The L-shaped living/dining room had a pass-through bar leading to the kitchen. There was a bathroom and two bedrooms down the hall.

One was for Pamela's mom, with a double bed, a dresser, and a chair. The other had a desk in the corner, like an office for Mrs. Jones, but the rest of the room . . . We stared. The twin bed for Pamela had a quilted spread, a white pillow with P-A-M-E-L-A in big green letters, a heart-shaped pillow, a fuzzy dog with big eyes and floppy ears, and a bunch of helium balloons tied to a bedpost. One read WELCOME! Another read LOVE YA! One even said MISS YOU. I could tell by Pamela's face that she was trying not to cry.

Mrs. Jones noticed it too because she said quickly, "For when you want to spend the night." And then, "I've got your dress right here." We were relieved that we could focus on something else as Mrs. Jones reached into the closet for the box from Nordstrom.

The dress was really hot—a black bottom and red lacy top with a red cloth rose at the waist.

"Detachable, of course," said Mrs. Jones. "Try it on, and we'll be the judges. Can I get you girls anything? Pepsi? Tea?" I'd noticed a bottle of beer on the counter when we walked in.

"I'll take some tea, thanks," said Elizabeth.

"Tea for me," I told her.

Pamela took the dress in the bathroom and closed the door. Elizabeth and I went back to the living area and sat demurely on the sofa, sipping the tea that Mrs. Jones brought us, the clinking of cups on saucers seeming too loud and out of place.

Pamela came out at last, and even barefoot, we could tell that the dress was just right for her.

"I can get it in a size smaller, but that looks about perfect to me," said her mother. "Do you like it?"

It was obvious Pamela liked it. She looked great. I think that what her mom was really asking was *Do you like me? Do you still love me? Can we start all over again?* Which is probably why Pamela just said flatly, "It's okay."

Mrs. Jones winced a little. "If you think it's too long . . ."

"I'll see," said Pamela, and went in the bathroom again to take it off. When she came back, she sat on the sofa between us, as though she needed protection on both sides.

"So!" said her mother, looking us over. "How's school?"

Pamela didn't answer.

"Pam's joined the Drama Club," I said, desperate to contribute something.

"Oh, Pamela, that's wonderful! You'd be so good onstage!" her mother said. "I'd come to every performance and clap like mad."

That was just what Pamela didn't want. "I'm not in anything, Mom," she said. "I'm just working backstage."

"But you liked the stage back in grade school!"

"That was grade school, and a lot has changed since then," Pamela said coldly.

"Only seniors get parts in the senior play," I said quickly.

"Well, when she's a senior, then," said Mrs. Jones, and lifted her teacup to her lips.

It was painful to watch. Painful to be there. Mrs. Jones was trying so hard, I could tell. But they were like magnetic poles. The closer she got to Pamela, the more Pamela backed away. Every lull in the conversation bothered them both, and Pamela's mother immediately tried to fill it with the first thing that came to her head.

I put that down in my mental notebook: One way to tell if you're really comfortable with a person is if you can be quiet together sometimes and not feel awkward. If you don't feel obliged to say something brilliant or funny or surprising or cool. You can just be together. You can just *be*.

Finally Pamela said we had to go and got up. She said we were going to study for a big test. She stood right there and lied to her mom, and we all knew it was a lie, even Mrs. Jones.

"Well then, I guess I'd better let you go," she said. "But you know you have a special place here now, Pamela. Whenever you want to come. In fact, you could have a sleepover right here! I've got an inflatable mattress!"

Pamela reached for her shoes, and Mrs. Jones brought our jackets.

"Thanks for the dress," Pamela said, tucking the box under her arm, and we moved toward the door.

"Anytime, Pamela," her mom said. "Anything at all I can do. Have a wonderful time at the dance. Tell Brian hello for me."

Once we got outside in the clear sharp air, it felt as though we'd been holding our breath in that apartment. We gulped in the rain, letting it splash on our faces, and it felt wonderful to get away.

"I can't stand it," Pamela said.

"She's trying, at least," said Elizabeth.

"It's all so phony!" Pamela went on. "'Come anytime!' she said. Ha! How do I know I wouldn't walk in and find some man there?"

The fact was, she didn't. Pamela had to trust. And there just didn't seem to be much of that left anymore.

When I got back to our house, Sylvia wasn't home yet. I went upstairs and started going through the clothes in my closet again.

The bridesmaid dress from Crystal's wedding wouldn't do, even if it had fit. It had "bridesmaid" written all over it. The backless dress wouldn't do either, even if it fit across the stomach. Definitely a dress for warm weather. Frantically, I began throwing all kinds of outfits across my bed, trying to see if I could make anything work.

"I'm home!" Sylvia called from downstairs, and I heard a door close.

"So am I," I called back. "Mayday! Mayday!"

There was a pause, and then I heard her footsteps on the stairs.

"Is that an SOS?" she called. Then, staring at my clothes-covered bed, "Are those coming or going?"

"The Jack of Hearts dance is in nine days, and I

don't have a dress that works. Some of them don't even fit," I said.

Sylvia came over and picked up a few hangers, looking the clothes over.

"Know what I think?" she said. "I think we need to go shopping."

"You mean, *buy* a dress?"

"Absolutely. And I know a neat little shop on Wisconsin Avenue over in Bethesda. Should we go tomorrow after school?"

"*Could* we?"

"It's a date," she said.

And there I was, shopping with my stepmom. I figured she'd go right over to the rack and start picking out dresses she thought would do, but she hung back and wanted to see what I liked. After we'd looked at a dress together, she'd comment on the color or the fabric, and when we'd narrowed the selection down to four, I set off for the fitting room to try them on.

I ended up with a midnight blue dress that had sort of iridescent stripes in the skirt. When I walked, when the material moved, the folds in the skirt looked blue and the creases black. It had short slit sleeves and a scoop neck, and the flouncy skirt flared at the bottom like a tulip, swishing as I walked.

I'd had my eye on a poppy red dress with a slit in back and an off-the-shoulder neckline. But Sylvia showed me how the polyester was stiff and didn't drape as well on my body, whereas the midnight blue dress, in rayon, almost seemed to dance with me, swaying where it was supposed to sway. When we discovered it was one third off the price, we beamed at each other.

"Oh, Sylvia, thank you!" I said. "Thanks for being you and not talking all the time and trying too hard."

"What?" said Sylvia.

As the saleswoman went off to wrap the dress in tissue paper, I told Sylvia about our visit to Pamela's mom and how everything the two of them said seemed to be wrong somehow.

"Hey, I'm a new mother, what do I know?" Sylvia said. "I'm just beginning to get the hang of it too. But I'll tell you this: You are one cool babe in that dress. Or should I have said 'hot'?"

"Cool will do," I said, and gave her a hug.

7

The-New-Girl-Who-Came-to-Learn-About-Sex

If Pamela hated visiting her mother, it was nothing compared to my dread of that "Our Whole Lives" class. I mean, I wouldn't even know any of those kids. I'd never gotten involved in any teen activities at church. I went to an occasional service with Dad and Sylvia, and that was it. I was going to stand out like a pretzel in a bowl of potato chips. Everyone would know everybody else, and I'd be The-New-Girl-Who-Came-to-Learn-About-Sex.

The class met on Sunday mornings in a downstairs room during the regular church service, Dad had told me. On this particular Sunday, I dressed in the most nondescript clothes I could think of—faded jeans, a beige T-shirt, denim jacket, ankle boots.

Dad and Sylvia weren't going to church that morning. They had their income tax forms spread out over the dining-room table and had set aside the day for that, so Dad just drove me over.

"How many kids are in this class?" I asked sullenly.

"I don't know," he said. "But this is the first year they've included sophomores, so I wanted to sign you up while I could."

"You mean they're mostly juniors and seniors?" I cried. "This gets worse by the minute!"

"There are a few other tenth graders, Al. You won't be the only one."

"Dad, I'm doing this just this one time for you," I said. "Don't ever sign me up for anything again."

"I promise."

At the church I got out of the car, closed the door, and shuffled along without saying good-bye.

When I walked in, there were about fifteen kids sitting around the room talking with each other, laughing. Some sat on the backs of the metal chairs, feet on the seat. Others sat on a table or windowsill. A few looked awkward and out of place, like me, like we'd rather be home cleaning the basement or something, but most of them seemed like they really wanted to be there. Like they were looking forward to it, even.

"Hi!" said a young woman with a name tag reading GAYLE. She was wearing jeans like mine and a white shirt, tucked in at the waist. "And you are . . . ?"

"Alice McKinley," I said, barely opening my mouth.

"Great! Make a name tag for yourself over there, and we'll get started in a few minutes," she said. She and a man named Bert were evidently the instructors.

I stuck my name tag to my denim jacket and slouched down in a chair, staring at the clock above the door. The second hand didn't even appear to be moving. *The longest day of my life,* I thought, and hoped I wouldn't recognize anyone from school. I didn't. I heard some of the kids talking as though they'd taken this class before. Could you fail it and have to repeat? I wondered.

Gayle and Bert didn't wait around to get things started, in case any of us decided to walk.

"Hi, everybody," Gayle said. "Welcome! I'm Gayle Linden and this is Bert Soams. We're both married, but not to each other, and we've been teaching this course for . . . oh, about seven years now, right?" Bert smiled and nodded. "Some of you are here for the second time, and that's exciting for us, because we never teach the class exactly the same way twice. There's so much material to cover, and the topics we choose will partly depend on you."

We had "check-in" then—we sat in a big circle and each of us said our name and where we went to school and stuff, and I was one of only three sophomores there. Nobody gave me "the look," though, so that was encouraging.

Bert handed out Xeroxed copies of the table of contents of the curriculum and divided us into smaller groups, where we were to decide which topics we wanted to cover: Intimate Communication; Sexual Orientation; Myths and Facts; Gender Issues; Values; Lovemaking. . . . It was a long list. I found myself in a group with a guy built like a wrestler—a senior, I'll bet—and a couple who were obviously bf/gf. He had his hand on her knee.

"Myths versus facts," the wrestler said. "I was in this class last year, and that's a good one."

"I want the one on communication," said the red-haired girl. "If you can't communicate, the rest doesn't matter."

We studied the sheet some more, discussed it a bit longer.

"What about you, Alice?" the boyfriend asked.

"They all look interesting to me," I said, opting for honesty. "But if one of them deals with putting a condom on a banana, I'd zap it."

They laughed.

When we got back in the circle again, Gayle said, "Someone might ask you—and you may have wondered yourself—why we offer this class here at Cedar Lane." She referred us to the blackboard, where she'd written some of the principles our church stood for and asked which ones we could apply to sexuality. *The inherent worth and dignity of every person,* read the first one.

"'Compassion,'" someone read aloud, studying the blackboard.

"'Acceptance,'" said someone else.

"'Respect' . . ."

"'Meaning' . . ."

Ho hum, I thought. Well, what could you expect from a church, after all? My eyes fastened on to the word *Respect.* If Dad had shown any for me, I wouldn't be sitting where I was.

"I think we get the drift here, that the sexual part of ourselves is deeply connected to our physical lives, social lives, spiritual lives . . . the whole nine yards," said Gayle. "There's a connectedness that we'll explore during these next couple of months, and Bert and I want you to remember that any-time—*any*time—you have a question, ask it! Interrupt if you have to!" She picked up a stack of papers and started them around the circle.

"There are no stupid questions in this course," said Bert. "Gayle and I go on the theory that for every person who asks a question, there are six or seven more who want the answer as much as he did."

The papers got to me. I took one and passed them on.

On the left side of the sheet was the figure of a female, all her sexual parts named, with a brief description of each: *ovary, cervix, clitoris,* and so on. On the other side was the male, with *testicles, penis, prostate.* . . . I'd been through all this before. The "Our Changing Bodies" unit back in seventh-grade health class, where we had to name all the parts. That "For Girls Only" class at the Y one summer. . . .

"And now for the fun part!" said Bert. "Everybody up."

I had that sinking feeling. We got to our feet.

"Gayle is going to go around the room taping a word on your back, one of the words you see here on the sheet," Bert continued. "Your job is to find out what word it is by asking for clues from each other, but the person you ask should answer in as few words as possible. For example, if I've got an ovary on my back"—we all laughed—"I can say to Gayle, 'Is it male or female?' and she can say, 'Female.' Then I have to move to someone else. 'I know I have a female on my back,' I can say"—more laughter—"and that person can say, 'Internal,' so I know it's something you can't see. Get the drift?"

Everyone was smiling, everyone but me, as Gayle went around taping sheets of paper on our backs.

"Ready?" said Bert. "If you guess correctly, you can sit down. Go!"

What was this? Musical chairs? What were we? Sixth graders?

I walked over to a girl who looked like she was rooted to the floor. "Can you help me out?" I asked.

"You mean as in, 'out the window'?" she joked. "Because that's just what I'd like to do."

"That too!" I said, smiling, and showed her my back.

"Male," she said.

"Thanks." I turned just as a tall guy with dark eyes was coming toward me. "Take a look," he said, turning so I could see his word. "I know it's female."

Clitoris, his sign read. Oh . . . my . . . God.

I stared at the paper in front of me to see what one-word clue I could give him. *The seat of female sexual pleasure,* I read.

"Um . . . pleasure?" I gulped.

"Got it!" he yelped. "Gimme a 'c' . . . gimme an 'l' . . . gimme an 'i' . . . ," and he continued until he'd spelled out the whole word. "Clitoris!" he yelped as my own face reddened, but everyone laughed. I laughed in spite of myself. He went over to the row of chairs and sat down. I should be so lucky!

I found another girl and showed her my sign.

"I know it's male," I said.

She thought for a minute. "Well, it's not exactly an organ. . . . It's sort of confusing."

Great! I thought. *I'll be the last one to guess what mine is.* The wrestler walked over, but before he could show me his back, I showed him mine. "I know it's male and it's not an organ," I said quickly.

"Hmmm," he said. "But it comes from an organ."

"Semen?" I guessed.

"You got it!" he told me.

Gratefully, I took a chair beside the other guy, and we watched while the rest tried to guess their words and, one by one, came to take a seat. Finally we were all rooting for the last person, who simply could not figure out his word.

"I've named every organ, male and female, on this whole paper!" he wailed.

Gayle laughed. "It's a joke, really, and it's not exactly sexual. In fact, it's not even on the paper, Kevin, so I'll give you a hint," she said. "It's both male and female."

"You mean I'm a hermaphrodite?" Kevin said as we burst into laughter.

"No. But everyone's got one," said Bert.

"Anus?" the guy bleated, and we howled. Gale

took pity on him and pulled the sign off his back to show him. *Belly button,* it read, and we cheered him for being a good sport.

I'll have to hand it to the church on Cedar Lane, they sure know what makes a good icebreaker. By the time the first session was over, we were comfortable saying those words out loud in a coed setting. Reading the definitions. Maybe the other kids had been comfortable with them before, I don't know. But the class didn't seem so threatening to me after that. I mean, what could we possibly have to do that would be more embarrassing than this? At the end of the session we had "checkout," and when it got to me, I told them the class was more fun than I'd expected.

When Dad came to pick me up, though, I put on my grouchy face.

"So?" he said pleasantly. "Was it better than you thought?"

"It was a slow two hours," I answered, which wasn't exactly true.

Silence.

"See anyone you know?" asked Dad.

"No."

More silence.

Finally I said, "Just what did you think I was about to do that made you enroll me in this class? I sure must lead an exciting life in your imagination. What was *Lester* doing at my age that's got you so worried?"

"Whatever it was, he didn't tell me," said Dad. "But he was leading an even more exciting life in my imagination than you are."

That afternoon, when Dad had fallen asleep on the couch with the newspaper over his stomach, Sylvia and I were in the kitchen making potato-leek soup for dinner, and I told her about the first session of "Our Whole Lives."

"Sounds fascinating," she said. "I wish I'd had something like that when I was fifteen."

I wondered how much I could ask. *Should* ask. Wondered how much I'd ask if she had been my birth mother.

"How much *did* you know when you were fifteen?" I said.

"Well . . . let's see." She was chopping leeks on the cutting board, moving her fingers slowly along the pale green stalks as the knife came down again and again. "I knew the mechanics, I guess you'd say. But I didn't know much about the sensations and emotions that go with sex, or how you talk with your partner about them. More like the art of brushing your teeth."

The phone rang just then, and I went out in the hall to answer. It was Aunt Sally, calling from

Chicago. She doesn't call as much as she used to because she doesn't want Sylvia to think she's interfering. But because she promised Mom she'd look out for us, she feels it's her duty to call now and then to make sure we're not malnourished or anything.

"Alice, sweetheart, how are things? I just got the Christmas decorations down and put away, and I said to myself, 'I'm going to call the McKinleys and see how they're doing.'"

"We're all doing okay," I said. "Sylvia and I are making soup, and Dad's taking a nap."

"It's good weather for soup," Aunt Sally agreed. "So what's new in your world?"

Did I dare? I wondered, beginning to smile. It is *so* easy to get her going. "Well, Dad signed me up for a course at church, and we had our first session this morning," I said.

"That's wonderful!" said Aunt Sally. "What kind of course is it? The Old or New Testament?"

"Neither one, actually," I told her. "It's called 'Our Whole Lives', and it's about sex."

I could almost hear the intake of air. "Your whole life is going to be about *sex*?" she cried.

"No, it's how sex fits into our whole lives, a part of who we are."

"Why are they teaching you this in *church*?"

"Because they want us to be responsible, caring

people," I said, beginning to sound like my father.

"Well, I certainly approve of that," said Aunt Sally. "As long as they don't go too far. The boys and girls aren't together, are they?"

"Yep," I said. "Coed."

"Oh my!" said Aunt Sally. "Well, what did you do in the first session?"

"I had to walk around for fifteen minutes with 'semen' on my back," I told her.

Okay, I went too far. I had to start at the beginning and explain the whole thing, and it would serve me right if Aunt Sally never wanted to talk to me again. But I decided that when it came time for me to put a condom on a banana, I'd keep that to myself.

Liz, of course, had made me promise that I would tell her absolutely everything—*every*thing—that went on in that class. So on the bus to school the next day, squeezed between her and Pamela, I told them as much as I could remember. Pamela was chiefly interested in whether any of the guys were hot.

"You probably would have gone for the guy with the word 'clitoris' on his back," I said.

Liz slid down in the seat. "I hate that word!" she said.

"Clitoris?" I asked.

She laughingly clapped one hand over my

mouth. "It just seems so . . . masculine or something. Like a tiny penis," she said in a whisper. "I don't even want guys to know I have one."

Pamela and I looked at each other, then back to Elizabeth. "What *do* you want guys to think you have down there?" I asked.

"A Keep Out sign," Pamela joked.

"No Loitering," I said.

"No Vacancy," Pamela added, and we started to giggle.

"No Parking," said Liz, getting into the spirit of things.

"Keep Off the Grass," I finished, and this time we howled.

"I just wish that sex was more like it was in the movies—the *old* movies—where women in gorgeous nightgowns kissed men in striped pajamas," said Elizabeth. "My grandmother said that when she was in high school, movies never showed men and women in bed together at all."

"They pretended they didn't even have double beds back then," said Pamela.

"Heck!" I said. "They pretended they didn't even have bodies!"

8

Home-Style

The night of the dance it was cold but not messy. You could see stars in the sky, even above the lights of Silver Spring. Pamela and Brian were double-dating with Penny and Mark, but Liz and Ross would be having dinner with Sam and me at his condo. When Sam drove over to pick me up, I thought he looked great in his gray pants and blue blazer, a shirt with cuff links, and a red tie.

Dad was upset because he didn't have any film for the camera, but Sam said that his mom was going to take pictures of us and that he'd make sure Dad got some.

"You look wonderful," Sam told me as he helped me on with the cape I'd borrowed from Sylvia. He leaned a little closer to the back of my neck. "Smell good too."

I should have! I was wearing Sylvia's perfume.

She had done both my fingernails and toenails and used a curling iron on the ends of my hair.

"Fantastic!" she said when she'd finished with me. I think that's the way Sam felt about me, too.

"What time is the dance over?" Dad asked.

"Eleven thirty," said Sam.

"You won't be going any place afterward, will you?"

"We don't plan on it," said Sam, deflecting the question.

"If there's any change, I'll call," I promised. "But we have to drop off Liz and Ross, remember."

Once in the car, I said, "I have to admit I'm a little nervous about dinner at your place."

"Why?" Sam asked, backing down the driveway.

"I don't even know your mother. She's going to a lot of trouble for us."

"Oh, she's a riot. She likes doing stuff like this," said Sam.

We pulled in across the street to pick up Liz and Ross. He'd come down on the train from Philadelphia that afternoon and taken the Metro to Silver Spring, where Elizabeth's dad picked him up. Sam got out when Liz and Ross came down the sidewalk, and I got out with him. Elizabeth was positively glowing.

"Hey, Alice!" Ross said, giving me a hug as he

approached the car. "Boy, do you look different than you did at camp!"

"And look at *you!*" I said. "Wow! You both look great! Sam, this is Ross, from camp last summer. Ross, Sam Mayer."

"How you doing?" said Sam, and opened the trunk for Ross's overnight bag.

When we were all back in the car, Ross said to me, "It was nice of your brother to say I could stay at his place tonight. I promise not to trash it."

Elizabeth was effervescent and chatty, and she filled Sam in on some of the things we'd done at camp. Ten minutes later Sam drove into the parking lot of his high-rise, and we took the elevator to the fourth floor. We walked down a corridor, made a turn, and there it was. Sam opened the door and we stepped inside. The room was dimly lit, candles everywhere, with soft music coming from a CD. The dining-room table had been set for four, and there was a long-stemmed rose lying across each plate.

"May I take your coats?"

We turned around to see a woman in a black turtleneck and white gloves smiling at us. She was sort of short and somewhat stout, but very official looking. I stared as I handed her the cape.

"Mom . . . Alice, Liz, and Ross," Sam said.

"Hello," she said. "I'm Martha, and I'll be your server for this evening." We laughed along with her as she pulled a chair away from the table, first for me, then for Liz, and we sat down. "Could I get you something to drink? We have Pepsi, apple juice, and V8."

"Uh . . . V8, please," I said, and the others gave their orders.

We turned and watched her head for the kitchen, then looked back at Sam. He was watching her too, and he grinned as he sat down to my left and Ross sat down by Liz.

"Humor her," said Sam. "She's enjoying herself."

I realized that the song we were listening to was Celine Dion singing "My Heart Will Go On." The candlelight flickered on Sam's face. "Happy Valentine's Day," he said to me.

I wanted to keep things casual. "It's officially not till next Monday," I said.

"Does that make any difference?" he asked, smiling.

Ross was wearing a tuxedo jacket and jeans and was taller than I'd remembered him. Liz looked the best, though, in her rose-colored dress. She was wearing blush of the exact same color, and I didn't wonder that Ross's hand was reaching for hers on the table. Sam put his hand over mine.

Mrs. Mayer came up behind me just then and set my V8 juice on the table. I pulled my hand away from Sam's so fast, I almost knocked over the glass.

When the first song ended on the CD and the next began, we started talking about our favorite singers, our favorite groups. Then Martha appeared again, without the white gloves this time, holding a notepad and pencil.

"Our appetizers this evening are crab bisque or spinach salad, and our entrées are chicken with mushrooms or Tuscan lasagna," she said. I decided she must have been a waitress in a previous life, she did it so well. It really was sort of like a restaurant, and certainly a lot cheaper for Sam, which was fine with me.

"This was really nice of your mom, Sam," said Elizabeth after Mrs. Mayer went back to the kitchen. "She put a lot of work into this."

"She's having a ball," said Sam. I wondered if Mrs. Mayer had ever done it for Sam and Jennifer when they were going together. Then I realized I'd ordered the spinach salad. *No!* Not with braces! Spinach was the worst! But I wasn't about to go after Martha and change my order.

Then the salads and soups arrived, and I hoped I wouldn't spill any oil on my dress. The worst part about a formal date is the dinner, I decided. I still remembered the night Patrick took me to his parents' country club, just Patrick and me, the summer before seventh grade. I was terrified. His folks drove us over, and I'd never even seen a dessert fork or a butter knife. After I got home, I'd opened my purse to find that I had stuffed the table napkin in there! Talk about embarrassing!

I speared a cherry tomato with my fork and sent a squirt of juice in Sam's direction. Everyone laughed. "Oh, I'm sorry!" I said.

"You only ruined my Ralph Lauren tie," Sam joked, and dabbed at the lapel of his blazer. And then I felt the spinach caught in my braces. When Mrs. Mayer came back with some rolls, I asked, "Could I use your restroom?" *Restroom?* Had I actually said *restroom*? In this *apartment*?

"Right this way," she said, and led me down the hall to the bathroom.

"You look lovely," she said, "and Sam's talked so much about you. Your father owns the Melody Inn, is that right?"

"No, he's the manager," I said as we reached the bathroom. I don't know what would have happened if this had been an emergency, because she went right on talking there in the hall.

"But he must have a wide range of musical knowledge to run a business like that," she said.

"Yes."

"Does he play an instrument?"

I ran the tip of my tongue over my braces, searching for spinach. "Flute, piano, violin . . . ," I said.

"Then he probably studied music in college. What university? I'm just curious. I have a lot of musical friends."

"Northwestern for his undergraduate, I think." I edged toward the doorway.

"So he did postgraduate work as well? Oh dear, I'm standing here talking and you need to get in," she said quickly. "Sorry." She gave me an apologetic look and went back down the hall.

Now, what was *that* all about? I wondered, closing the door behind me. Talk about the third degree! It was all about Dad. Our family. His education. His status. I felt as though I had just been interviewed for a position in a company. Future daughter-in-law or something. But maybe it wasn't all that different from Dad asking questions about Sam.

I checked my teeth in the mirror, and sure enough, it looked as though I'd lost a tooth where a hunk of spinach had blacked it out.

There was a little basket lined with a gingham cloth on top of the toilet tank. It held an artfully arranged disposable toothbrush and paste, tampons, hair spray, dental floss, and aspirin. I had the feeling this was just for Liz and me. I used some of the dental floss.

When I came back to the table, the entrées had arrived.

"Enjoy!" Martha said. When she returned to see if everything was okay, we told her that her food was wonderful.

"Thank you," she said, laughing. "I'll be sure to tell the chef."

Somehow I managed to get through the meal without sliding the chicken breast onto my lap. I remembered to cut up only the next bite of meat, not the whole piece. Not to blot my lip gloss on the linen napkin, just to dab at my mouth. Not to use my own knife to help myself to the butter. Honestly, Dad and Lester and I ate like pigs at home, I thought. Maybe now that Sylvia was living with us, I'd learn some social graces. I had to think about every move I made.

"I like your dress," Sam told me.

"Sylvia helped choose it," I said. "She has great taste in clothes."

"What's it like having an English teacher for a mom?" he asked.

"Weird," I said, and joked, "About the same as having a waitress for a mom, I guess."

It must not have sounded right, because I had expected Sam to laugh and he didn't. I added quickly, "I hope she knows how much we appreciate this."

"I'll tell her," Sam said.

Mrs. Mayer removed our plates when we had finished and delivered little chocolate cakes in the shape of hearts for dessert. She and Sam exchanged smiles.

"Terrific meal," I told Sam. "She should open a restaurant."

"She really could too!" said Sam. "And she could decorate the walls with all the people she's photographed." He motioned toward one whole wall of the living room, which I hadn't noticed before because the light was so dim.

"She's a photographer too, then?" Ross asked.

"Yeah. She does freelance for some of the local newspapers," Sam told us. Then he turned on some lights and gave us a tour of their living room. You could tell he was proud of his mom. He could have been her press agent, the way he showed us around. There was a photo of Chelsea Clinton, Sean Penn, the mayor of New York, a scientist at the National Institutes of Health. . . .

As we moved around the room Sam kept one arm around my waist, and every so often his lips brushed my cheek. I liked that. I liked Sam. I think I would have enjoyed the evening a little more if his mom weren't around, though.

When we got to a photo of the Redskins' coach, Ross and Sam started talking football, and Liz and I went down the hall to the bathroom together. I pointed out the little basket of "necessaries" on top of the toilet tank.

"This is so weird," I said. "I'm glad you guys are here."

"I think his mom's kind of nice," said Liz, combing her hair.

"She is. I just . . . I feel like she's watching me through one-way glass or something."

"That's what Jennifer said," said Liz.

"What?"

"What Jennifer said when she dumped Sam. I heard her telling Charlene. She said she felt that Mrs. Mayer was along every time they went out."

"What did she mean by that?"

"I have no idea," said Liz. "I wasn't even supposed to hear."

"You never told me."

"I didn't know you'd be going out with Sam. And besides, why should what *she* felt affect you?"

Liz was right, I supposed. And Sam really was being sweet to me. So was his mom.

"You think we should leave a tip?" I asked, motioning to the little stack of paper guest towels.

Liz grinned. She took the eyeliner pencil out of her purse and wrote *Thank you, from Alice and Liz* on one of the towels and left it for Mrs. Mayer on the sink.

"It was a pleasure meeting you," Mrs. Mayer told me when she brought my cape, and gave my hand a squeeze.

"The meal was wonderful, and so are your photographs," I said.

As we went back down to the parking garage, Liz and Ross lagging behind to kiss, I asked Sam, "No dad in the picture?"

"No," he said. "They separated a long time ago. Never divorced, but I hardly ever see him. He's in Florida. Sort of weird, huh?"

"I guess so," I said.

"I asked Mom about it once, and she said they respect each other too much to get divorced but they don't love each other enough to live together. Figure that one out."

"I wouldn't even try," I said.

9

Alone Together

The gym had been transformed into a red and white fairyland. Red, white, and pink streamers formed a ceiling over the polished floor. A strobe light went on every now and then, creating a large circle of light in front of the band, with "snowflakes" swirling around and around inside it. When dancers moved into the circle, their bodies were covered with tiny dots of light.

Artificial Christmas trees lined both sides of the dance floor. They had all been sprayed white, with red and pink hearts dangling from their branches. The faculty chaperones hung back by the punch table, but every so often a few came out to dance. I remembered how upset I used to get when I saw Sylvia Summers dancing with her old boyfriend, Jim Sorringer, back at our junior high school dances.

"Has anyone seen Pamela?" I asked when I

spotted Jill and Justin. And then I saw Pamela's red top across the gym. She was gorgeous, of course, and Brian already had his hand too far down on her back.

Sam had his arm around me when the next number began, and we danced out into the dark as the lights went down a notch. It was different from dancing with Patrick. When I leaned against Patrick, my head was against his chest. When I leaned against Sam, our cheeks were side by side. That was okay too!

I could see Karen and her date and caught a glimpse of Penny and Mark. Everything seemed different with the snow-covered trees, the little lights, the music, the way we looked, all of us dressed up, so sophisticated. I turned my face toward Sam, and we kissed as we danced, our feet scarcely moving at all.

When the band took a break, Liz and I went down to the girls' locker room to check our makeup. One of the teachers was there offering tissues and combs and any help she could give. Pamela came in, balancing on a new pair of stiletto heels.

"Hey, hot stuff!" Liz said.

"Ross is one magnificent hunk!" Pamela told her. "All the girls are looking at him. Be glad he's in Pennsylvania, or they'd be lining up at his door."

"Yeah, lucky me," said Liz.

I leaned toward the mirror and reapplied my lip gloss, then my eyeliner, vaguely conscious of the girl next to me in the purple dress with the low-cut neckline. She was holding a mascara brush, flicking up her lashes, her dark hair piled on top of her head.

The girl on the other side of her said, "Marcie, who's your date? I didn't see you come in."

And the girl with the mascara brush said, "A guy from band, Patrick Long."

I tried not to stare. Did I know her? One of the school brains, I figured. I watched out of the corner of my eye as she removed a contact lens and put it back again. Then I realized she played first flute in the school band. She was probably about as perfect a girl as Patrick could get, I thought. Was I jealous? A little, I guess. *I* was his first choice, though, I reminded myself.

Giving my hair a few quick stabs with my comb, I went upstairs to find Sam. A fast number was just ending, and the lights were dimming again.

Sam smiled at me. He put one arm on my waist and with his other hand, held mine close to his chest. I snuggled against him. We were dancing toward the band when I noticed that some of the couples had stopped near the edge of the strobe-lit circle, their faces turned toward the couple dancing there in the light.

I wondered if it was Patrick and Marcie. Sam wasn't even aware of the couple or the others watching. His eyes were closed, and he pulled me tighter to him as we swayed from side to side to the music.

As we kept turning, though, the couple attracting all the attention came into view, and I could see two figures dancing alone, their noses almost touching as they looked into each other's eyes.

It wasn't Patrick and his date. It wasn't even Jill and Justin or Faith and Ron. It was Lori and Leslie, each wearing dark pants and dressy black tops, and they danced as though there were no one else in the whole wide world except them.

We talked about that when the dance was over. Some of the other kids were going out to eat, but we'd had our dinner, and Dad expected me home. I didn't want him calling me on my cell phone. We drove to Lester's. Ross got his overnight bag out of the trunk, and we waited while Liz went over to the side steps with him and they kissed in the shadows. Sam and I looked away.

"What'd you think of Lori and Leslie?" asked Sam.

"I think they looked great," I said.

"It's hard to watch sometimes, though," he said.

"You think so? *I* think it's hard to watch Jill and Justin sometimes—the way they're all over each other. You just want to say, 'Get a room!'"

Sam smiled and pulled me to him, and *we* kissed. He grinned at me. "You think it feels that good when lesbians kiss? Lori and Leslie?"

"Why not?"

"What about gay marriage?"

"Nobody told me they were engaged!" I joked.

"In general, I mean." Sam always manages to turn things into a serious conversation.

"Well, some people are always saying how promiscuous gays are, and yet when they try to settle down with one partner, they can't make it legal," I said.

"You've thought about the question, then?"

"I've thought about Lori and Leslie and how rotten they've been treated by some of the kids," I answered.

"I suppose you're right," said Sam. "But I take marriage pretty seriously."

Were we really having this conversation? I wondered. I didn't want to ruin a wonderful evening. "Well, I won't be thinking about marriage for a while," I told him.

In the light from the streetlamp I could see the twinkle in Sam's eyes. "Not at all?"

"Oh, now and then. Off and on," I said, and

laughed. "How do you know I want to get married at all?"

"You mean, you wouldn't?"

"That's light-years away. I've got five or six years of college ahead of me, Sam. What about you?" I asked, meaning college.

"I think about it," he said, meaning marriage.

Elizabeth came back to the car reluctantly and got in, and I saw Lester open the door to Ross at the top of the side stairs.

"It must have been hard to say good night," I told Liz.

"It was," she said, "but he's coming over tomorrow before he goes home."

After we let her out at her house, Sam pulled in our driveway. I was nervous. This was such a formal date. After the work Sam and his mom had gone to in making a nice evening for me, I felt I ought to invite him in. I didn't know if I wanted Dad and Sylvia to be waiting up or not.

Sam turned off the ignition.

"Would you like to come in for a little bit?" I asked. "I think we've got some sparkling cider in the fridge."

"Sure," said Sam.

I got out my key as we went up the steps and opened the door. I made enough noise to let Dad know I was home and heard a toilet flush upstairs.

"Just want you to know I'm home and Sam's here," I called.

"Okay," Dad called back.

"Come on out to the kitchen," I told Sam. I got down two glasses and found the cider behind the milk carton. It was a fancy bottle with a cork instead of a cap. I found the corkscrew, and Sam took off his jacket. He uncorked the bottle and poured the cider.

As he lifted his glass he said, "To us," and clinked his glass against mine.

We took them back to the living room and set them on the coffee table.

"I really enjoyed this evening," Sam said as we sat down together on the couch, his mouth against my ear.

"So did I," I said.

"In fact," said Sam, "I've wanted to go out with you since the first day I saw you in eighth grade."

"Really? What was I doing?"

"Eating lunch," he said.

"Eating *lunch*?" I gasped. "And that got your attention?"

"You were talking to Patrick, actually. And I wished it was me." He ran his hand up and down my bare arm and kissed the side of my face.

"Well, now it *is* you," I said, and turned toward

him. He kissed me, just brushing my lips with his. The bulb from the floor lamp shone directly in my eyes when we pulled apart, and Sam reached behind him and turned it out so that our only light came from the kitchen.

"Much better," he said.

Everything was like I was doing it for the first time. The kissing, the touches. Except it wasn't as awkward now as it had been at the beginning with Patrick. That first time Patrick and I kissed, it was so excruciating. I couldn't wait for him to leave. But it wasn't like that now. Now I wanted Sam to stay. I wanted it to last. And more than that . . .

Sam moved in slow motion. Everything he did was slow. I thought about the movies where the man and woman suddenly grab each other and start swallowing each other's tongues, practically. It was different with Sam. His lips touched mine lightly, making me eager to press mine against his. His hands caressed my hair, my shoulders. I don't really know how long we were there on the couch, half sitting, half lying down . . .

The floor creaked above us.

"Al?" Dad called down the stairs.

"Yes?" I answered.

"You work tomorrow, remember."

"All right."

Sam grinned at me and stood up. "That's my cue, I guess," he said. He drew me toward him, and we kissed again. "We won't be in such a hurry to come inside next time."

10

Pamela's Story

Sylvia tapped on my bedroom door before I was awake the next morning, waited a few seconds, then opened it a crack. "Alice?"

I was down in a deep dark well, so full of sleep and oblivious to place and time that my head felt like one of those toy slot machines: You pull a lever and wait while pictures whir and spin in the windows. Eventually, they began to line themselves up, and I was conscious of Sylvia standing beside my bed.

"Alice," she was saying, "I really hate to wake you, but Elizabeth called."

I struggled to open my eyes. The lids were just too heavy. I could feel the movement of the mattress as Sylvia sat down beside me, but I was drifting off again, lulled by the softness of my pillow that somehow became Sam's shoulder in my dream.

Now Sylvia was gently massaging my back. "Liz has invited you to brunch at her house around eleven."

Sam's shoulder disappeared and became my pillow again. "What?" I murmured.

"Ross is coming over before he goes back to Philly, and Mrs. Price thought it would be fun to invite the three other girls who were at camp with him last summer."

My lips moved. "What time is it?"

"Ten twenty. I've let you sleep as long as I dared. Ben said you don't need to come into work until one today."

Now my eyes were open. It was Saturday, the busiest day at the store. "Really?" I said. "It's okay with him?" I rolled over so I could see Sylvia's face. Her hair was wrapped in a towel, and I could smell the conditioner she uses. "I could sleep for days," I said, drawing my knees up into a fetal position.

She smiled. "Have a good time last night?"

"Yeah, the dance was great." My eyes closed, opened again, closed. . . . "Is anyone in the bathroom?"

"No. It's all yours."

I got up then and staggered into the shower, then shocked myself awake by turning on first the hot water, then the cold . . . hot . . . cold. . . .

• • •

Pamela and I got to Elizabeth's at the same time. Gwen was already there, and Ross was sitting at the table holding a glass of orange juice when we came in.

"Only eleven o'clock on a Saturday morning and we're awake!" Pamela cried.

"Awice!" Liz's little brother called when he saw me. I swooped him up in my arms and flubbered the side of his neck before his mom whisked him away so we could have the kitchen to ourselves.

There were scrambled eggs and bacon and coffee cake on the counter. We helped ourselves, then sat around the table. Liz was on Ross's lap at one end, arms around his neck.

"Did Les drive you over?" I asked Ross.

"No. Liz's dad came and got me. Thanks again for asking Les if I could sleep over there," Ross said. "They gave me a blanket and pillow and, man, I was out!"

"Have you heard about next year?" Pamela said, lifting a pecan off a piece of coffee cake and popping it into her mouth. "The school's replacing the Jack of Hearts dance in February with a Sadie Hawkins Day dance in March—girls' choice."

I remembered we had talked about that at a newspaper staff meeting.

"Why?" asked Elizabeth.

"There'll be an article in *The Edge* next week," I

told her. "A lot of kids feel there are too many formal dances. It's too expensive. So next year there'll be two informal dances—Homecoming and Sadie Hawkins—and two formals, the Snow Ball and the prom."

"I can live with that," said Gwen. She was wearing a white fleece sweat suit, but there were still glittery silver beads woven among the dark circular cornrows on her head. She looked like a goddess.

"Did you have a good time last night?" I asked her.

Gwen gave me a rueful smile. "Mostly I danced with Yolanda. One of our dates kept going outside to smoke, and the other one kept hanging around the punch table, looking for something to eat." We laughed.

"You weren't the only girls dancing together, I noticed," said Ross.

"Yeah. Lori and Leslie looked great. And as far as I can tell, nobody hassled them," I said.

"Yeah, but did you see what happened to that girl—what's her name?" said Gwen. "That really thin girl who dresses all in black and wears the bright red lipstick?"

"Faith?" I said. "Why? What happened?"

"I'm not sure, but she was down in the locker room with a torn sleeve and a big welt on her arm. She'd obviously been crying. She told the teacher there that she'd fallen on the ice."

"What ice?" I said.

"Yeah, that's what I wondered," said Gwen.

"It's that boyfriend of hers," I said angrily. "He treats her like dirt, and she keeps going back for more."

"There are other guys who would ask her out if she gave them half a chance, I'll bet," said Liz. She was caressing Ross's ear with one finger.

"And quit dressing like a witch," said Pamela.

"The thing is," I mused, "even if she dressed differently and three other guys asked her out, she still might choose Ron. Weird, isn't it? Like she *needs* to be knocked around."

"Love," said Pamela disgustedly.

"Love!" Liz responded, bending down and kissing Ross on the lips. We all gave a loud dramatic sigh and broke into laughter.

"Speaking of which," Ross said, turning to me, "I met your brother's girlfriend."

I lowered my fork, and the scrambled eggs fell back onto my plate. "Girlfriend?" I said.

"Yeah. At his place. They were having coffee when I got up this morning."

Pamela and Liz and Gwen all turned their eyes on me, but I was still staring at Ross.

Lester has had plenty of girlfriends, but as far as we could tell, he hadn't had a current girlfriend for some time now.

"She . . . was there this morning?" I asked.

Ross looked around uneasily. "Yes . . ."

"So . . . she was there all *night*?" I asked.

"Uh-oh," said Ross. "Erase! Erase!"

"What was she *wearing*?" Elizabeth demanded, and we knew that if she was in her robe, Lester was toast.

"I refuse to answer on grounds that I may incriminate somebody," said Ross.

I could believe Les would have a girlfriend staying overnight, though he'd never said that he had, but I could hardly believe he'd do it with Ross there.

"What's she like?" I asked.

Ross shrugged. "I don't know. Nice . . ."

Nice? Is that all he could tell us?

"Well, what does she look like?" asked Gwen.

Ross shrugged helplessly. "Attractive. I don't know . . ."

What is it about guys, I wondered, that they never notice the details? "Well, what *did* you notice?" I asked him.

Ross thought about that a minute and tried to hide a smile. "I think she was drinking her coffee black. No, maybe she put sugar in it, I'm not sure." I think even Elizabeth could have strangled him at that point.

"Well!" Pamela said to me. "Looks like you need

to have a little chat with your brother, Alice. I mean, we want *information* here! This is a biggie!"

"Hey, leave me out of this," said Ross. "It was nice of him to let me sleep on their couch. Besides, he *is* an adult, you know."

I knew that, but somehow it's hard for me to accept that Lester is grown up. Maybe you *never* look at your own brother as grown up, I don't know, even after his hair turns gray, which Lester's has not.

We hung around Elizabeth's talking about all the fun we'd had at Camp Overlook, about when we were getting our driver's licenses, and what we planned to do the coming summer. I didn't feel so bad not knowing what I was going to do because nobody else seemed to know either.

Sylvia drove me to the music store a little before one. I was tempted to tell her that Lester had a new girlfriend who had spent the night with him. But then I decided that if Lester was ever going to confide in me and treat me like an adult, I had to be someone he could trust. So unless he brought it up himself with Dad and Sylvia, my lips were sealed. Just wait till I got him alone, though!

At the Melody Inn, Marilyn wanted to hear all about the dance. I told her about my dress and about Sam and the dinner his mom made for us. About Lori and Leslie and how Gwen had seen Faith crying in the girls' locker room.

"It's possible she *could* have fallen," Marilyn said. "You don't want to jump to conclusions."

"Then she falls an awful lot," I said.

"Well, if her boyfriend is abusing her, the one thing she can count on is that it will get worse," said Marilyn. "I've had a couple of girlfriends in that situation. Control freaks keep upping the ante. The more she gives in to that, the tighter the screws. She should break it off while she can."

"Yeah, try to convince Faith of that," I said.

That evening, this being Valentine's Day week-end, I decided to hole up in my room with my CD player so Dad and Sylvia could have some privacy. I called Gwen and Liz and Pamela in turn, just to talk. We had to go over every detail of the dance, things we couldn't quite say in front of Ross.

"Don't ever date guys from your own church," Gwen said. "They're more like brothers than boyfriends."

Oh, I don't know about that, I thought. I didn't think I'd ever feel like a sister to the guys in the "Our Whole Lives" class.

Elizabeth was still dreamy over Ross. "You

know," she said, "some high school romances *do* last. My aunt married her high school sweetheart."

This was the second time that marriage had come up in a conversation recently—first Sam, now Liz. "You aren't thinking about *marriage* already, are you?" I asked her.

"No, but we have to think about it sometime," she said.

Pamela had the most to tell because Brian had his driver's license, and he had done the driving.

"Where did you go after?" I asked.

"You mean before or after we took Penny home and dropped off Mark?"

I thought about that a moment. "Well . . . both."

"We went to a Mexican restaurant in Bethesda, and then we took Penny home. Then Mark," she said.

"And then?"

"We parked."

"*Yeah?*"

"And did . . . whatever." Her eyes turned impish.

"I didn't know you liked Brian that much," I said.

"Oh, he's okay. You don't have to be wild about someone to do whatever." She laughed. "And *he* had a good time, anyway."

"Pamela!"

More laughter. "Okay. So I gave him a hand job."

"I don't think I want to hear this."

"Of course you do. You asked. It's a good idea to practice on somebody you *don't* care a lot about so that you'll know how to do it on somebody you *do* care for."

"*What?* I don't believe this!" I said. But I did. "How did it . . . ? I mean, did he . . . ask you to do it or what?" I was still trying to picture it in my head.

"He just unzipped his pants and put my hand there. It didn't take long, but it's kind of sticky, if you want the truth."

"You know, you make it sound like you put your hand on a doorknob, for all the emotion you put into it," I told her.

"Don't lecture," Pamela said warningly.

"I'm not. I'm just surprised, I guess, that it . . . well, didn't mean any more to you than that."

"But it's sort of exciting to see how easily you can turn a guy on," Pamela said. "You get a guy begging for it, he'll do almost anything. It's kind of amazing!"

"So what did he do for you?" I asked.

"Nothing. Not that he didn't try. But . . . jeez, it's *Brian*! I've known him forever. I'd probably end up laughing. If I'd wanted sex, though, I'll bet he'd have done it. I *know* he would."

"A hand job *is* sex, Pamela."

"You know what I mean. So how did things go with Sam? Tell me about that dinner. What was it like?"

"Well . . . his mom was dressed like a waitress. She took our orders and everything. She really went all out. There were even long-stemmed roses on our plates."

"Is she for real?"

"I guess so. And the song she was playing on the CD was 'My Heart Will Go On.'"

"Alice, that is definitely creepy," Pamela said.

"Oh, it was for Valentine's Day, after all. Liz and Ross seemed to have a good time. Sam says his mom enjoys that kind of thing. She's a photographer, and her photos are all over their living room. It's just, well . . . if it had been somebody else's mother, I probably would have been more comfortable."

"You know what I think?" said Pamela. "It's her way of checking out the girls Sam likes."

"You think?"

"Why else?"

"Maybe she really *is* just being nice."

"Yeah, and maybe I was just being nice to Brian." Pamela laughed. "Anyway, Liz looked great, didn't she?"

"Yes, and I love seeing her so happy with Ross," I said.

"Me too. If I didn't like her so much, I'd be jealous," said Pamela.

I lay in bed that night thinking about what Pamela had told me about Brian. About practicing on guys you didn't like so you'd know what to do with guys you *did* like. *The inherent worth and dignity of every person.* It was impossible not to remember that. It was impossible too not to think of Faith and Ron.

11

Questions

At the "Our Whole Lives" class the next morning Gayle had written another word on the black-board: *Intimacy*. Bert was explaining how being intimate is not a single act, but everything from just watching a sunset with someone to talking about personal things to having intercourse. Then he asked us to name every possible act we could think of that expressed intimacy or sexual feeling between two people. As we called out words Gayle wrote them on the blackboard.

"Kissing," said a girl.

"Talking," said another girl. "I mean, really saying how you feel without hurting the other person's feelings."

"Hugging," said someone else.

Back rubs, holding hands, foot massages, oral sex, mutual masturbation . . .

The thing about the class at Cedar Lane is that

things I'd hardly thought of doing before were okay to talk about there. Words I wouldn't say aloud to most people. But Gayle and Bert didn't even blink.

Gayle brought up the fact that our bodies are ready for sex long before our particular society is ready for us to have it. In some cultures, she said, girls are married off as soon as they start menstruating, and early sex and childbirth are the norm. But in our country, where parenthood is delayed until long after the body is physically ready for sex, our problem is what to do about sexual feelings before we're ready for marriage.

The *third* time in the span of one weekend that somebody had mentioned marriage!

One of the guys told about a party his friend had gone to where everyone was doing something sexual, short of intercourse, to someone else. All in the same room.

A few kids moaned.

"Okay," Gayle said. "What's wrong with that picture? Anything?"

"It's . . . like they're onstage. Performing," said one girl. "I mean, how can you feel anything for anybody if it doesn't matter who it's with and you've got an audience?"

"Well, it's safer than having intercourse," said a guy.

"Can't argue with that," said Bert.

We thought about it some more.

"I'd think there would be about an eighty percent chance for humiliation," said the tall guy I'd talked to the week before.

"Yeah, but if you just look at the whole thing as a practice session . . . ," said someone else.

"I don't think I want to be somebody's guinea pig," I offered, thinking of Pamela and Brian.

Gayle nodded encouragement, but that was all I wanted to say. That was another thing I liked about the class: You could decide for yourself just how deep you wanted to get into a topic. I wasn't ready to tell Dad, though, that—surprise! surprise!—I liked the class.

Lester's car was waiting at the curb when it was over. I slid into the passenger seat.

"So have you found out everything you wanted to know about sex but were afraid to ask?" he said.

"Never mind *me,* Lester, let's talk about *you!*" I said, glad to have this chance with him alone.

"Yeah?" He swung the car around, and we headed back toward the street. "What *about* me?"

"Well, I know you're an adult, but—," I began.

"Who are you? Rip van Winkle, just waking up from a long, deep sleep?" he asked.

"I mean, it's not any of my business, but I *was*

sort of surprised that you'd have a girlfriend there right next to Ross," I said.

"What?"

"Next *door* to Ross, I mean. In the next room."

"I don't know what you're talking about, Al, but somebody here is hallucinating."

"The *woman,* Lester! You were having breakfast with a woman the morning after our dance."

"Having breakfast is not a sexual activity," he said.

"Now, look. I can put two and two together," I told him. "If she was there at breakfast, she was probably there all night."

"So?"

"*So?* Why didn't you *tell* me you had a new girlfriend?"

"That was George Palamas's fiancée. She woke up before George did, so she came out in the kitchen to have coffee and I happened to be there. Is that a crime?"

I stared at him. "You didn't sleep with her, then?"

"Of *course* not! Are you crazy?"

I smiled and leaned back against the seat. "Lester, you have restored my faith in the decency of man," I told him.

"And you have confirmed my view that all fifteen-year-old girls should be locked up in an insane asylum until the age of twenty-one," said Lester.

"Just tell me this," I said. "What were you doing at my age that's got Dad so worried that he signed me up for this class?"

"Well, let's see," said Les. "Fifteen for me was the Age of Embarrassment. I had a bet with some girl in my science class—I don't even remember what it was about—but the agreement was that if I won, she'd let me see her breasts. I won, and we sneaked off to the band room after school, but I couldn't get her bra unfastened. I think I finally jerked on it so hard that it bent one of the hooks, and there we were when the custodian found us."

"What happened?" I asked, trying not to laugh.

"He asked for our names, he was going to report us. I said I was Morton Magee and the girl was Molly Malone or something. You never saw two people clear out of a room as fast as we did."

"Poor Lester," I said.

"I vowed I would practice until I could unhook a girl's bra in two seconds flat, but I didn't have any bras to practice on. So . . . ," Lester paused, as though unsure of whether to tell me the rest.

"So?" I said encouragingly.

"So . . . I ordered a bra from the Sears catalog,

and Dad opened the package before I got home. He never quite got over it."

I laughed and so did Lester.

"If you order anything by mail," he said, "make sure it's not a jockstrap."

After lunch I'd just spread out my books on the bed when Sam called on my cell phone.

"So how are you?" I asked, bunching a pillow up under my head.

"Missing you," said Sam. "Want to go somewhere?"

"I can't," I told him. "There was the dance Friday night, and I worked Saturday and went to church this morning. I am *so* behind on my homework."

"Any way I can help?" he asked.

"Not really. I've got a lot of catch-up reading to do and a ton of algebra."

"Well, I miss you," he said again.

I laughed. "It's only been two days."

"What about after school tomorrow, then?"

"I've got a stage crew meeting."

Sam sighed. "You're too busy."

Strange, I thought. That's what I always said about Patrick. "I know," I told him.

"Tuesday after school? If I can get Mom's car?"

"Okay. Tuesday," I said.

A half hour later I was in the middle of an equation when Sam called again. He always calls my cell phone number so he won't disturb Dad and Sylvia. I had thought I understood the problem I'd been working on, but when Sam interrupted, I lost my train of thought.

"Sam . . . ," I said.

"Can't help myself. If I can't see you today, I can at least hear your voice."

"I was right in the middle of an algebra problem," I said.

"Well, if it's between algebra and me, which one would you choose?" he asked.

"You, of course," I told him. "But I don't get any grade for studying Sam."

When my phone rang a third time about an hour later and I saw Sam's number, I didn't answer. And finally, when the ringing stopped, I turned the phone off.

When the crew met in the rehearsal room after school the next day, Mr. Ellis hadn't come in yet. The guys were sitting on the tables at the back talking about a hockey game, and the girls—Molly, Faith, Charlene, Pamela, and I—sat in a circle of chairs across the room.

We'd been talking about the Jack of Hearts dance, and suddenly Molly came right out and asked Faith what Ron did to make that bruise on her arm that kids had been talking about. That's Molly! But I was glad she'd asked.

Faith fumbled with the strap on her purse. I think she had a bruise on her cheek, too, but it was covered with so much makeup, it was hard to be sure.

"He really doesn't mean to hurt me," Faith said in the soft breathy voice you'd know anywhere.

"Well, you could have fooled me!" said Molly. "He doesn't mean to hurt you, over and over again?"

"It's just—," Faith began, and stopped. Then she tried again. "You may not believe this, but it's because he cares about me so much!" Pamela rolled her eyes. "He gets so jealous, he can hardly stand it."

"Yeah?" said Molly. "So what happened this time that set him off?" She was relentless.

"I danced with someone else. The thing was, I didn't know it, but Ron set me up to test me. He told a guy to ask me to dance and said he'd give him five dollars if he could get me out there in the spotlight. So there I was, Ron had disappeared, and this guy came up and said Ron would be back in a little while and had asked him to look out for me, and did I want to dance? So I did. And Ron was watching all the time. I should have known better. He is so insecure."

"*He's* insecure?" I spluttered.

Faith sighed. "Oh, I know what you think of him," she said. "But . . . I mean . . . after he loses his temper, he's so sweet to me. Really! When he saw what he did to my dress and my arm, he had tears in his eyes." Faith turned to Molly. "He's so sorry! He's apologized a million times. He just hasn't learned to trust me yet, and he can't control his temper."

Molly shook her head. "If a guy ever hurt me once—just once, Faith—it'd be the last time I went out with him."

"I know," Faith said. "But what can I do? I love him!"

Underneath all that black and white and red makeup, Faith is really pretty—a sort of high-cheekboned, skinny girl. She's got the most beautiful teeth I ever saw—perfectly even and white as the moon. And you wonder why she would settle for someone like Ron, like he's the most necessary person in her life, as essential as air.

Mr. Ellis came in then and passed out lists, detailing what each committee needed to do for the spring production. Harry and Chris and I went over the design for the set and talked about what kind of wallpaper we should use and where exactly the windows should go. Faith went over the list of props with Pamela.

Before the meeting was over, the door opened, and Ron came in. He sat down in a chair along one side of the room. He was holding a single rose. *Long-stemmed roses must be "in" this season,* I thought. When Faith turned and saw the rose, she got up and went over to him, and they kissed. *See?* she seemed to be saying to us. *See how much he loves me?*

I looked at Molly as we picked up our jackets. "What do you think?" I said.

"I think we've heard that song before," she answered.

I didn't have any courses with Sam this semester, and we had different lunch periods, too. The only thing we did together in school besides walk together in the halls—and Sam went out of his way to meet me between classes—was the weekly staff meeting for *The Edge.* This was probably why he called me so much. It always seemed to take Sam three or four calls each evening to tell me whatever he wanted to say.

On Tuesday after school I told Pam and Elizabeth that I was riding home with Sam, and I met him in the school parking lot.

We kissed. I guessed we were going to be one of those couples I'd always looked at so enviously when I was in seventh grade—older couples who walked down the hall with their arms around each other, hands in each other's hip pockets. Couples who stood by the drinking fountain and hugged.

It had all happened so fast with Sam, partly, I guess, because I'd known him before, so he was already a friend. And partly because he made me feel as though I was the only one who mattered in the whole world. I had the feeling he would do anything I ever asked.

The front seat of Sam's mom's car was a bench-type seat, not bucket seats, which meant I could snuggle up next to him, and I guess I was surprised at how easily I took his kisses. Maybe after all those months without a boyfriend, all those weeks at camp last summer watching Liz and Ross together, I was just plain hungry for making out, like you get a craving for mocha chocolate chip ice cream or something. Or maybe I was beginning to feel that I had something special here in Sam.

This time his hand caressed the back of my neck as he tipped my face up toward him. When the kiss was over, his hand slid down inside my unzipped jacket, inside the top of my shirt, pushing it aside and baring my shoulder. Then he kissed my shoulder. I shivered, not because I was cold.

"You want to go to Starbucks?" he said.

No, I was thinking. *I want to sit right here in the school parking lot till you kiss my other shoulder too.*

"Um . . . I don't know," I said.

"Silver Diner?" he asked. He must have been hungry.

"Okay."

We kissed again, and this time, when we slowly pulled apart, Sam let his hand slide from my collarbone to my breast—just for a moment—and then he pulled away. My whole body went goose bumps.

"Seat belt," he said into my hair.

The second nice thing about a bench seat is that there are three seat belts in front, one for a middle passenger, which meant I could sit right next to him. But Sam had proved he was a careful driver, and we didn't try anything dumb when the car was moving.

"Don't ever get bucket seats," I said, and he smiled.

At the diner we got the last booth in the row, away from a noisy table near the door. I ordered hot chocolate, and Sam ordered Sprite and a hamburger. I told him I'd pay the bill since Sam had to buy gas whenever he used the car.

"Question," said Sam as I stirred my cocoa, then blew on it, watching the creamy marshmallow topping slide back and forth. "If you were in love with a guy—"

"An anonymous guy?" I asked, teasing.

He chuckled and ate the pickle off his bun. "Well, yeah. Let's make him anonymous. How much would you do for him?"

I raised one eyebrow. "How much would I *do* for him? Is this a how-far-would-I-go question?"

"I wasn't thinking of sex," said Sam. "Well, that's a lie, but actually, I had something else in mind. I really meant, well, would you move to another town for him, for example?"

"You mean, if we were going to be married and he got a job in another city? Sure. It would have to be a mutual decision, though."

"Okay. Would you marry him if he . . . lost a leg or an arm?"

"Well . . . certainly! I wouldn't leave somebody I loved because of that."

"Would you change your hairstyle? Your weight?"

"I don't know. Depends on how controlling I thought he was being."

"Your religion?"

"My God, it *depends*! How much would *you* change for a girl you loved?"

"All of it," said Sam.

It was strange in a way, nice in a way, but a little bit scary at the same time to be talking like this with a guy. Like we had a future together, I mean. I'd never told anyone but my dad that I loved him. Well, maybe Lester, too, in a weak moment. I don't think I'd ever said "I love you" to Patrick. I'd never said it to Sam. Yet here we were, talking as if . . .

"It's just that I'm pretty serious about love," said Sam.

"Well, so am I," I told him. And thought, *I guess*.

12

Wheels

On Saturday at the Melody Inn, I answered the phone around eleven, and a girl's voice said, "Alice?"

It was so familiar! Not Gwen or Liz or Pamela . . . "Rosalind?" I said, my old friend from grade school.

"Yep," she said. "How you doing?"

She had surprised me back in October by walking in the Melody Inn to buy some music for her brother, and we'd promised we'd get together sometime and have lunch. Bill used to play in a little band with Lester when we lived in Takoma Park. They called it the Naked Nomads, and sometimes Rosalind would come along when they practiced so she and I could do stuff together.

"I'm great!" I said. "How about you?"

"Even greater," said Rosalind. "Guess what? I've got my license. Tell me what time you go to lunch, and I'll pick you up."

I squealed. "Really? My lunch break is twelve thirty."

"How long you got?"

Dad was unpacking some boxes with David across the room. "It's Rosalind," I called over to him. "How long can I take for lunch?"

"A half hour if you're leaving at five, an hour if you stay till six and help me file the new sheet music," he said.

"Deal!" I told him. And to Rosalind I said, "I have to be back by one thirty."

"See you!" she said.

It was funny about Rosalind. She had been every parent's nightmare because each time she came over, we'd get into trouble. Something always went wrong when Rosalind was there. She had an imagination big enough for both of us. Lester said that the one good thing about moving from Takoma Park to Silver Spring was that we were getting away from Rosalind. Now he was living back in Takoma Park and Rosalind had found me in Silver Spring!

I watched her pull up at twelve thirty sharp, right by the fire hydrant in front of the store. It was an old car—older than Sam's, even—sort of a nondescript gray-green. I could see Rosalind smiling at me before I went outside. Everyone in her family has a round face, with mouths that turn down at the corners even when they're laughing. But this time that mouth didn't seem to turn down at all, her smile was so wide.

Giggling, I slid in beside her.

"Rosalind!" I cried, and leaned over to hug her.

"Can you believe I've got my own set of wheels?" she said, checking the rearview mirror and slowly pulling out into traffic.

"You mean it's yours?"

"Yeah. Bill got another car and sold me this one for two hundred dollars. About all you can say for it is that it runs. But, hey, it's mine!"

"So where are we going?" I asked.

"I brought lunch," she said, motioning to a sack from McDonald's in the backseat. "Why don't we drive back to the old neighborhood and you can see your house."

"Why would I want to do that?" I asked.

"They painted it pink," said Rosalind.

"Pink?"

"Like cotton candy," said Rosalind, and off we went.

It really feels awesome to be riding in a car with someone you used to walk to the playground with. I mean, back then I wasn't allowed to go farther than a furniture store in one direction and the school in the other. And suddenly here we were in a car with a tank full of gas, and we could have headed for Miami if we'd wanted. Well, not really, but it felt like we'd sprouted wings. No bus schedules, no stops, just go! *Freedom!*

I marveled at how Rosalind had slimmed down some, how shiny her hair was. Yet every time I glanced her way, I was glad for each little mannerism that reminded me of the Rosalind I used to know. I was looking for every familiar detail I could get, yet I loved being in a car with her. Roots and wings. I wanted them both.

The day was mild for February—high fifties, maybe—and we even rolled down our windows a little. The sun was warm on our legs.

"So tell me everything!" I said. "Everything that's been going on."

"Wait till I get off Georgia Avenue and out of traffic," Rosalind said. I waited while she changed lanes, carefully checking her side mirror, her rearview mirror. I noticed how she came to a gentle stop at lights, not racing up and slamming on the brakes. When it's your car, you treat it like a baby, I guess. I wished this was me—my own key, my own car. . . .

Silver Spring soon became Takoma Park, and Rosalind pulled into a little play area and parked near the jungle gym. We took our chicken sandwiches and shakes over to the swings and sat there in the sun, eating lunch. I slipped a couple of dollars in her pocket for mine.

"You still volunteering at the zoo?" I asked. I remembered her telling me that last fall.

"Yeah. And I'm working at a vet's," she said. "I do a little of everything. The office is closed today, though, because he's out of town."

"You're good at that, I'll bet," I said. "You always loved animals."

"Nothing's changed there. I may even go to veterinary college if I can get in," said Rosalind. "What's new with you?"

I pointed to my mouth. "Braces," I said. "Dad married my English teacher, you know, and Lester's living in an apartment with two other guys."

"Where?"

"Here in Takoma Park, actually. You want to see where?"

"Sure."

We finished eating, threw our trash in the garbage can, and got back in the car. Rosalind drove me by our old house next door to the Sheaverses. It *was* pink.

Remember the time we made that snow cave and it fell in on you?" said Rosalind.

"You kicked it in!" I said, poking her arm. "Do you remember the night we helped Les get ready for the prom? And the block party, with the Naked Nomads?" We laughed.

"I used to drive your brother nuts," said Rosalind.

"And you probably still would," I told her.

I directed her to Maple Avenue, then on to the big yellow house on a side street. "Here we are." I pointed to the steps leading up to a side entrance. "They live on the second floor."

Rosalind pulled up in front of the house and stopped. Her eyes took on that mischievous look I knew so well. "I'll bet Lester thinks he's finally rid of me," she said. "Let's go in."

"We can't!" I said. "We can't just come over here without calling first."

"Wanna bet?" said Rosalind, and got out of the car.

I started laughing. There was nothing to do but follow along and try to control the damage. When Rosalind gets an idea, she's unstoppable.

"Lester's not even here," I said, relieved, as she started up the walk. "His car's gone. He's working."

"So I can still see his apartment," said Rosalind, and went up the steps. "Who are the other two guys?"

"George Palamas and Paul Sorenson. Look, Roz, you're on your own. This was your idea."

Rosalind knocked. It was a full minute before anyone came, but then Paul opened the door. Tall and thin, he looked like a younger version of Ichabod Crane.

"Yes?" he said, and then he saw me. "Well, hi, Alice. I'm afraid Les isn't here."

"We know," said Rosalind. "But I'm a friend of the family, and I just wanted to see his new digs."

Paul stared at her, then at me.

I tried not to laugh. "Rosalind, Paul. Paul, Rosalind," I said. And then to Paul, "You'd better let her in. She won't leave unless you do."

Paul grinned a little. "Okay. Look around. We haven't cleaned up, though."

"I'll feel right at home," said Rosalind.

Paul went down the hall, and I noticed he closed his bedroom door as well as George's. George Palamas was in an old pair of sweats on the couch, looking at the stock market pages of the *Post*. A half-eaten bowl of cereal sat on the end table beside him. He looked at us quizzically.

"We're not staying," I said quickly. "Rosalind, this is George."

"Hello," said George, and went back to the business section of the paper.

"Okay," I said to Rosalind, giving her a quick tour. "Living room . . . kitchen area . . . bathroom . . . bedrooms . . . and this one is Lester's." At least he'd left his door open. I wouldn't have let her go in if he hadn't. The bed was unmade, of course.

Clothes on the back of his chair. His desktop was covered with papers and books, and there were stacks of books, like termite hills, all over his floor.

Rosalind looked round. She began to smile. She took one pile of books and set it on top of another. Carefully, she lifted a third pile and balanced it on top of the second. When she lifted still another pile, I said, "Rosalind!"

But she managed to get that balanced too.

"Don't breathe," she said, tiptoeing carefully over to the desk. She took out a blank sheet of notebook paper and wrote, *Rosalind was here*. Then she placed it on top of the stack of books, we said good-bye, and laughed all the way back to her car.

I thought Lester would be gunning for me when he came for pancakes the next day. But he surprised me. He didn't come at all.

"You think we should call him, Dad?" I asked.

"What for? Where is it writ that a grown man has to have pancakes with his dad every Sunday morning?" Dad said, slipping a couple of golden circles onto my plate.

"Nowhere," I said, "but he can usually smell pancakes all the way from Takoma Park."

"The spring semester is always the busiest," Dad said. "He's got a lot on his mind."

I had a lot on my mind too. When I wasn't thinking about our school trip to New York in April, I was thinking about my driving lessons. If Lester thought he could get out of his promise by just not showing up on Sundays, he was mistaken. But meanwhile, I had another "Our Whole Lives" class to get through.

This time the subject was sexual readiness, and we each got a handout with questions to ask ourselves before engaging in sexual intercourse. Questions like, *Do I really trust my partner completely? What will I do to prevent pregnancy?*

One of the guys read another question aloud. "'What makes me feel I want to have intercourse right now?' Is this for real?" he asked. "Is there ever a time I *don't?*"

After the list of twenty questions the handout read, *If you cannot answer all of the above with confidence, you are not ready for sexual intercourse.*

"Jeez!" a dark-haired girl said. "After answering all these questions, I'd be too *tired* to have intercourse!" And we laughed.

The thing was, the questions were good ones, and to answer them all, you had to know yourself really well. You had to know your partner really well. Your family. *His* family! I'll bet half the people engaged to be married couldn't even answer all those questions!

"How do you tell a guy you like that you don't want to have intercourse?" somebody asked.

"Or how do you tell a girl?" said a guy. "Sometimes it seems she expects it."

We spent the rest of the session just talking about that—how you turn down a girl without making her feel she must be unattractive; how to turn down a guy without sounding like a prude.

"How about if *you* want sex and the girl says she doesn't? But she's afraid she's hurt your feelings. How can you convince her you're okay with that?" said another guy, and we discussed that too. It all seemed to boil down to respect—really listening to what another person has to say.

It was strange in a way that when I started the class, I was thinking primarily of me. *My* body. *My* sexuality. How it would be for me. And I could see that the focus was going to be on the other person as much as yourself.

Liz and Pamela weren't the only ones interested in what we talked about there. Sam wanted to know about it too. I didn't tell him everything, though. I didn't get too specific. The thing about Sam, I discovered, is that he sort of jumps to conclusions. If you even mention a subject, that makes it a big deal. So when he asked what this session had been about, I said, "All the things you need to think about before you start a serious relationship."

"All I think about is you," said Sam.

"That could be a problem," I told him.

13

Hello, Tracy!

The next Sunday Les didn't come over either.

- "I could always run over to his place with a Care package and see how he's doing," Sylvia suggested. "Chocolate chip cookies and homemade bread."

"He has two housemates, and if anything's wrong, they'd tell us," said Dad.

On Wednesday night, though, Lester called and asked if we had enough dinner for four.

"How does beef stroganoff sound?" Sylvia said, and I take it the answer was affirmative.

I was setting the table when Les came in. We eat in the kitchen unless we have company.

"Where've you been, the South Pole?" I asked, giving him a quick once-over.

"Busy," said Lester. If there was anything different about him, it was that he looked more alert and alive. I figured he'd finished the big paper he was working on and was feeling good about it. As we all sat down and Sylvia passed the salad, Les said, "Just wanted to tell you that I've met someone really special."

If we were dogs, three sets of ears would have pricked up all at the same time. Our eyes were all focused on Lester.

"Aha!" said Dad. "That explains it!"

Les grinned and helped himself to the Stroganoff. "I met her six weeks ago in a statistics course. Then we started having lunch together, and for the past few weeks we've been going out."

Was this it? I wondered. Was Les really and truly in love?

"What's she like?" I asked. My ears felt like satellite dishes, ready to pick up his slightest murmur.

"Smart, caring, funny, attractive . . ."

"I can't wait to meet her," said Dad, smiling. "What's her name?"

"Tracy Freeman. Majoring in special ed. We've had some long walks, long talks. . . ."

"Now, that *does* sound serious!" said Sylvia.

Why was he telling us all this? I wondered. Lester had never told us much about his girlfriends before.

"Some people," said Lester, "you never get to know them completely. And others, like Tracy, you just spill out your guts to the second time you meet."

"Guts don't sound especially romantic to me," I said.

He only laughed.

"What does Tracy like to do when she's not in school?" asked Dad.

"Loves to travel. Likes the theater. Does some watercolor painting. She's not much into sports. I offered to give her tennis lessons, but I don't think she'll take me up on it. Anyway, I think you'd like her. And did I mention that she's African American?"

I stopped chewing. So did Dad and Sylvia.

"No, you didn't mention that," said Dad.

"George and Paul think she's great. We've had her over for dinner a couple of times, and one time she cooked for us. Great cook too."

Sylvia smiled. "Les, is there anything *not* perfect about Tracy?"

"Well, as I said, she needs tennis lessons," he told us.

Later, after Les went home, I looked at Dad and said, "What do you think? I've never heard him talk about any other woman this way except Lauren."

"I think Les has a good head on his shoulders and is old enough to know what he's doing," said Dad.

• • •

I began to see Patrick around school with the girl he took to the dance—the girl who plays first flute in band—Marcie Bernardo. They didn't kiss in the halls like Sam and me, but a couple of times I saw Patrick with his arm around her. What do the really brainy kids talk about when they're making out? I wondered. Quantum physics? Magnetic poles? Solar flares? The big bang?

Sam was definitely more of a hands-on kind of guy—always touching my arm, my cheek, my neck, my back—and I liked it. Too much, perhaps. I wanted more. Gayle talked about that in one of my "Our Whole Lives" classes too—how that's the way we're *supposed* to feel. That's how bodies are *supposed* to react.

One of the topics we'd chosen for discussion was lovemaking, and the Sunday we talked about that, just to take some of the awkwardness out of it, we came to the session to find that Gayle and Bert had borrowed road signs from the state highway department and had propped them around the room: STOP; YIELD; DANGEROUS CURVES; SLIPPERY WHEN WET; SLOW; RESUME SPEED; MERGE; PROCEED WITH CAUTION. . . . It made us laugh.

Cedar Lane Church is pretty liberal, I guess, but when you come right down to it, I think Gayle and Bert's attitude about us having sexual intercourse

was more on the order of STOP or SLOW than PRO-
CEED WITH CAUTION.

I got on my computer later and invited Liz
and Pamela to my chat room. Pamela thought
the road sign idea was a riot when I told her
about it.

> **Lovliz13**: i can't believe all you talk about,
> alice. if you ever marry anybody from that
> class there won't be any surprises left
> **pjhotbabe**: surprises are out, liz. nobody
> expects surprises anymore
> **Loveliz13**: well that's too bad cause there
> should be something left to discover
> **AliceBug322**: i sorta feel that way too
> **pjhotbabe**: well maybe you'll find out
> your new hubby wears lifts in his shoes
> **AliceBug322**: or he has a glass eye or
> wears a toupee
> **Lovliz13**: what if i'm wearing a padded
> bra? is that false advertising?
> **pjhotbabe**: absolutely. even shoulder
> pads count
> **AliceBug322**: maybe nudists have it right.
> when a nudist proposes, he's already in-
> spected the merchandise, top to bottom

The third Sunday in March, Lester brought Tracy

to dinner. Sylvia baked a ham, and I made a pound cake.

We had the table set in the dining room, and from the window I watched Lester and Tracy get out of the car—Les opening the door for her and Tracy, in a red jacket and gray slacks, grabbing his arm as she stood up. The wind whipped her scarf around her face so that it almost blew away, and she laughed as Les caught the end of it and tucked it down inside her jacket.

Dad opened the door. "Come in! Come in!" he said.

"Tracy," Les said, "this is my dad. Sylvia . . . Alice . . . this is Tracy."

"Hello," Tracy said, unwrapping her scarf, and Dad took her jacket to hang in the closet. "Quite a wind we've got out there!"

Her eyes were heavy lidded, and she had a dimple in one cheek but not the other. Her skin was the color of cinnamon, and her figure was very much like Sylvia's, only a little fuller. She smiled around at us expectantly.

"We're so glad to have you," Sylvia said. "Please come in and sit down. Dinner will be ready in a few minutes. There are cheese straws you can nibble until then."

As we sat around the living room Tracy said to me, "I hear you've got Les booked for the month of April. Driving lessons."

"Really?" I said. "He told you that? The whole month?"

"Depends on whether or not you're a slow learner," Lester said.

"I didn't even try for my driver's license till I was eighteen," Tracy confessed. "There was no way I was going to get a car in high school, so I just let my dad drive me everywhere. But college put an end to that, thank goodness."

Dad asked about her major then, and after Sylvia called us to the table, Tracy told about growing up in D.C. and how she always got season tickets to Arena Stage.

What I was watching for, though, were the little gestures that meant they were in love. The quick glances, the occasional whisper, the smiles, the touching—all the stuff couples do. Tracy was probably too shy. You're careful when you're in your boyfriend's house for the first time and his parents are staring at you. You feel awkward, like I had at Sam's. But we liked her from the moment we met her, and after she and Les left around nine, Dad said, "Well, one thing I'll say for Lester: Tracy's a great improvement over the last two."

"Which two were those?" asked Sylvia.

"Eva, the sophisticate . . . ," said Dad.

". . . and Lauren, one of his instructors at the U," I finished. "Lester almost cost her her job."

"They just weren't right for him," Dad said.

"And Tracy?" said Sylvia.

"I don't know," said Dad. "No one knows all the things that go into a relationship. Sometimes not even the people themselves."

"Not even you and Sylvia?" I said, teasing.

Sylvia smiled at Dad. "We're still learning," she answered.

On the bus the next morning Liz asked, "Who was that woman getting out of Lester's car last night? I was sweeping off our steps when they pulled up."

"Lester's new girlfriend," I said.

"Girlfriend?"

"Tracy Freeman." Then I turned to Pamela and said, "She's African American, and Les wanted us to meet her."

"Wow!" said Pamela. "Is he serious?"

"He's crazy about her, I think," I said.

Pamela thought about that a minute. "Dad told me once that if I ever brought home a Latino or a black, he wouldn't let either one of us in the house."

"Sight unseen?" I said.

"Right. Without knowing anything about them at all," said Pamela.

"So I guess Koreans and Greeks and Canadians

and Russians and Eskimos are okay?" I commented.

"You know what I mean," said Pamela. "He's prejudiced against anyone who's not a one-hundred-percent white made-in-America male." And then she added bitterly, "So he marries a one-hundred-percent white made-in-America female, and look where they are now: He's holed up in front of the TV every evening eating Stouffer's, and she's in an apartment in Wheaton, and he won't let *her* in the house either."

She slid down in the seat, tipped back her head, and closed her eyes. "I can't *wait* to get out of here. I can't wait for New York."

"Gwen said she officially signed us up as roommates," I told them.

"It'll be just like a college dorm!" said Elizabeth.

"It'll be *freedom*!" said Pamela. "And let me tell you, I am going to *party*!"

14

Getting Ready

The next two weeks were totally crazy. *Father of the Bride* was playing the last weekend in March and the first weekend of April, and now there were rehearsals every day after school. The cast had been chosen in February, and at that time the stage crew needed to have only a few pieces of furniture in place so the actors could get the feel of where the doorways were and where the couch and chairs would go.

But now the crew had to see how far to the left and right the scenery should extend and try out different lighting schemes to find the ones that made skin tones look most realistic. The cast members sometimes rehearsed well into the evening and the backstage crew was supposed to attend as many rehearsals as we could. When the first two performances went off with only small glitches with props or lighting, we thrust our fists in the air backstage and grinned at each other before the final curtain.

At least Pamela came regularly and did her back-stage work, even though I knew her heart was onstage with the actors. There were times I caught her watching from behind the curtain, her lips moving as she mouthed their lines.

That could be you, Pamela, if you could get your old spunk back, I thought.

The second weekend of performances is almost more nerve-wracking than the first because you're supposed to have ironed out all the kinks. Whatever mistakes we made the first time around, Mr. Ellis said were learning experiences, but by the third performance, we had no excuse, and were relieved it went smoothly.

I don't know about the final performance, because I came down with a zinger of a sore throat. It hurt horribly to talk, and Dad said no way was I going to leave the house. Not only did I miss the final performance, but the cast party as well. Half the fun of being part of the stage crew is the cast party, but when you feel as bad as I did, you just want to stay in bed and try not to breathe too hard.

I heard Sylvia explaining it over the phone to Pamela when she called. I heard her tell Pamela to go on to the cast party without me, and to please explain to Mr. Ellis. And I heard her tell Pamela that I'd said if she didn't go to the cast party without me, I would tell the whole crew about the time back in sixth grade when Pamela called a Volvo a vulva in front of the class.

Sylvia's tinkly laughter filled the hallway and I knew Pamela was laughing too. Then I spent the rest of the evening hunkered down under the covers feeling sorry for myself—wondering what the kids were saying at the party, and who was making jokes, and who came in costume and whether Ron let Faith come at all.

Like a true friend, Pamela called me the next morning.

"I know it hurts to talk," she said, "so I'll do it. Everyone missed you—really. All the guys asked about you—Harry, Chris—and Molly had everyone sign a program for you. I'll bring it over when you're better."

"Did Ron . . . ?" I croaked, wincing as I tried to talk.

"Yeah, the jerk was there. He kept his arm around Faith all evening, until it began to look more like a chain instead of an arm. He is such a loser! Every time Faith even *talked* to another guy, Ron would nuzzle the side of her face to distract her. Listen, get better, okay? I'll call again tomorrow and see how you're doing. And hey! *I* had a good time, believe it or not."

When Sam called to see how the last performance had gone and Dad told him I was sick, it was only an hour before he arrived at our house with some of his mom's soup—turkey something-or-other. Do mothers have this stuff just sitting around or did she make up a fresh batch just for me? I wondered. He wanted to come up to see me but Sylvia told him he'd better not, I might be contagious, and I was grateful. I would have locked myself in the bathroom if they'd let Sam see me looking like this.

Anyway, Dad took me to the doctor on Monday for a throat culture, and by Wednesday, when I felt tons better, he said I could go back to school. The culture turned out to be negative for strep, but it didn't do my homework for me, and I had two days of catching up to do.

Liz and I were barely home from school that day—I'd stopped by her house to play with Nathan—when Pamela phoned.

"You two have got to come over," she said. "You won't believe what I got in the mail just now."

"Can't you tell us?" I said over Elizabeth's shoulder.

"No," came Pamela's voice. "You've got to see for yourselves." And she giggled.

I had been sitting on the couch, pretending to

be reading as Nathan ran around and around—through the hall, then the kitchen, the dining room, the living room—and each time he'd pass the couch, I'd reach out and try to grab him. He'd shriek with delight.

"You're wearing me out, buddy," I told him as I slipped my jacket on again. "Just wait till next time! I'll catch you for sure!"

"We're going over to Pam's, Mom," Liz called.

Pamela lives a few blocks from us and when we got to her house and she opened the door, she waved a newspaper in my face. "Just arrived from my cousin in New Jersey," she said. "The *Village Voice.*"

"Yeah?" I said.

"It's the weekly newspaper of Greenwich Village. Anyone who's cool, wild, and outrageous reads the *Village Voice*. This will tell us exactly where to go." And then, with a sly grin, she said, "Now, don't have a spaz, Liz." Pamela flung open the newspaper to a full-color photo double spread.

I yelped and Liz covered her eyes momentarily as rows and rows of crouching women exposing their backsides came into view, with captions such as TWO GIRL SPECIAL and HOT TRANS SEX and BEST BODY SHAMPOO IN NYC, all with phone numbers.

"Oh . . . wow!" said Elizabeth. We giggled as we

sat down together on the couch to look some more.

"Hey, Alice, this is you," said Pamela, pointing to the headline of one ad: LOCAL GIRLS GO WILD.

"No, this is *you*!" I said, pointing to HOT NASTY GIRLS. And then we found the perfect one for Elizabeth: OVER THE KNEE SPANKING AND MUCH MORE. We howled.

"Good thing Dad's not home or he'd cancel my trip," Pamela said. Slowly, she turned the pages while we gaped and commented and wondered aloud how a woman could allow herself to be photographed "this way" and "that way" and "o'm'God, look at *that* way!"

"Okay, now we've got to get serious," said Pamela, grabbing a felt-tipped pen. "Clubs! We've got to find some clubs."

Liz was holding the paper now, propped against her thighs, feet on the coffee table. "Here's one," she said. "'Shadow-dancing barkeep performs nude in upstairs sultan's tent.'"

"Mark it!" I said. Pamela drew a large circle around the ad.

"What about this?" I suggested. "'A three-dollar cover gets you into the Tuesday night rubfest, where you can gawk at funky hipster chicks dancing on well-stocked bars.'"

"We won't be there on a Tuesday," said Pamela.

"How are we going to get into any of these places?" I asked.

"We'll worry about that later," Pamela declared, making another circle on the paper. "Whee! Look at this one. 'Well-oiled studs do karaoke in the raw'!"

"Yes!" Liz and I said together.

"And this!" I said. "'Be participant or observer as you sip your drink under the stern tutelage of whip-bearing waiters'!" So much for the dignity and worth of every human being.

"Pamela, how are we going to *do* any of this?" Elizabeth asked. "They've already told us there's lockup each night."

"I've got a plan," said Pamela. "After lights-out we—"

"Lights-out? This isn't camp," I objected.

"Lights-out, lockup, whatever. We put on our robes over our regular clothes and go down to the front desk. We tell them we smell smoke up on our floor. There will be a lot of confusion, and they'll send people up to check. They might even set off the fire alarms. That's when we slip out. And nobody can blame us for leaving our room if we smelled smoke, right?"

I thought about it. "Okay. We're standing outside. What do we do with our robes?"

"Yeah, that's the part I haven't figured out yet. If

we go down in our jackets, though, they won't believe us about the smoke."

"I know!" said Elizabeth. "Let's each bring an old robe we don't want anymore, and after we get outside, we'll give them to a street person."

We gave each other a high five.

"Okay, then what?" I asked.

"Then we get in a cab and go to one of these places. Bring lots of money."

Elizabeth looked thoughtful. "What time is this supposed to be? The school's got our evenings planned. We'll have parent chaperones breathing down our necks till we go to our rooms."

I was afraid there was a hitch somewhere. "Yeah, we've got to get away for a whole evening, Pamela," I said.

Pamela chewed at her lip. She appeared to be thinking so hard, her brains hurt. "Plan B," she said. "Forget the robes and the smoke. I'll have my cousin call me on my cell phone and tell me her mother just died. I've got to go to her house for the night and comfort my relatives."

"What about us?" asked Liz.

"I have to bring my two best friends to help. Three, counting Gwen. There are a lot of relatives."

"Pamela, you know that'll never fly," I said.

She threw back her head in exasperation. "Okay,

plan C. Forget the smoke, the robes, and my dead aunt. We'll crawl out a window or something. Where there's a will there's a way! The thing is, we have to be committed to having a night on the town. If we're just going to buckle under and spend a perfectly good New York night in our room, then we might as well stay home. Are we in this or not? Are we going to give up the best chance we ever had to do something really wild together?"

"No," I said, feeling adventurous and daring. "We've got to at least try."

"I agree," said Liz. And added, with a melodramatic flair, "Even virgins have to cut loose now and then."

At the next newspaper staff meeting we were supposed to be talking about the feature article each of us was to write for a coming issue of *The Edge*. What we were doing instead was checking out who was going to New York and who wasn't. Sam, of course, had signed up as soon as he knew I was going.

"When I go to New York, it won't be with a school group," said the junior roving reporter. "It'll be me and my buds with tickets to Madison Square Garden."

Tim, our assistant editor, and Tony, our sports

editor, were going to go, but Jayne, the editor in chief, wasn't. She said she always went up with her aunt, and they took in a couple of plays over a weekend.

I sure haven't traveled much. I mean, some people my age have been to France and Spain. I've been to Chicago and Tennessee. Big deal. That's why New York City seemed a lot more exciting to me than it did to some of the others.

"Last year my aunt and I did *three* plays in one weekend," said Jayne.

"I'd spend the whole time shopping if I could," said another girl. "The stores stay open practically all night long, and you can buy absolutely anything you ever wanted."

"Hel-lo!" said Miss Ames, our sponsor. "We have a paper to put out here! Jayne, what features do you have lined up so far?"

Jayne snapped to attention and started down the list. When she got to me, I said, "I thought maybe I could do a feature on what students worry about the most."

"Grades!" said Tim.

"College," said Jayne.

"Sex," said Tony, and I wondered if I only imagined it or if he glanced at me when he said it. We all laughed.

"That's an interesting topic, and you seem good

at drawing out people's feelings, Alice," Miss Ames said. That really pleased me. "I wonder how you can sort out the flip answers from the real McCoy, though."

"I think she ought to keep the kids anonymous," said Tim. "She needs to promise them that she won't use their names in the article."

"Yeah. Go for it," said Sam.

They all agreed. Usually we try to use as many students' names as possible in each issue because everyone likes to see their names in *The Edge*. But this time we'd leave them out.

When the meeting was over and we were gathering up our stuff, Tony said, "You want a ride home, Alice?"

And before I could open my mouth, Sam said, "I'm taking her. I've got the car."

"Okay. See ya," Tony said, and went out.

Sam gave me a puzzled smile.

"What?" I said.

"Doesn't he know I took you to the dance?" he asked.

"I don't know," I told him. "What does it matter?"

"I guess it doesn't," said Sam. "I just wondered if he had designs on you."

"Designs?" I said. "What is he? A tattoo artist?"

"Okay, the hots," said Sam.

I just laughed. "You'd have to ask Tony."

Sam put his arm around me as we walked out to his mom's car. "When we get to New York," he said, "I want you all to myself."

Why didn't that make me all tingly and excited? I wondered. In a way it did. But all Sam and I had talked about so far was sitting together on the bus going up and back. I also had big plans with the girls. Now I was stuck with a balancing act: How much time to give Sam? How much attention to Pamela and Elizabeth and Gwen? I wanted a real feeling of getting away, and now I felt as though I would be dragging my life in Silver Spring along with me.

Somehow it must have registered on my face. When I didn't respond, Sam gave my waist a little tug. "You okay with that?" he asked.

"Well, they've got us on a pretty full schedule," I said.

"We can always find a way to slip out," said Sam.

"Okay. But I'm rooming with Gwen and Pamela and Liz, so part of the time I'll be with them," I said.

He looked disappointed. "I thought we could do lots of things together. I mean, that was the point of going, wasn't it? For me, anyway."

"I could be with you here, Sam. We don't need to go to New York for that."

"I mean, away from everybody."

I tried to laugh it off. "When we're in your car, we're away from everybody."

"Not as much as I'd like." He grinned and nuzzled my ear.

15

Problem

Les had a few hours to spare on Saturday afternoon, so Dad let me off work early for my first driving lesson. In Dad's car. His new car. Dad had
said he'd give me a few lessons himself if he had
to but that all his gray hair had come from teaching Les to drive. If he had to teach me, too, his hair
would probably fall out.

Everyone under eighteen who applies for a
license in Maryland has to go through thirty hours
of driver's ed, but *no*body wants to look like a
complete nerd at the wheel, especially if other students are in the car with you. We all want to look
cool, as if we've driven before and are just taking
the course because we have to. With Dad's permission to miss work, I was planning to sign up
for four Saturday mornings plus two evenings a
week after we got back from New York.

I grinned excitedly as I slid into the driver's seat.

Les helped me adjust the side and the rearview mirrors and pull the seat up until I felt a comfortable distance from the wheel. I turned on the ignition. There's something about the sound of the engine engaging and the whole car beginning to vibrate and purr that makes you feel so powerful. Excited and scared both, because Dad's car was only six months old.

"Okay," said Les. "Put the car in reverse and back slowly down the driveway."

I put my hand on the gearshift and moved it to the R. The car began to roll. I panicked and slammed my foot on the brake. Lester's head jerked backward.

"Easy, Al!" he yelped.

I inched my foot off the brake, and the car began to move again.

"Watch for cars," Lester said.

I braked again, more gently this time. A car was coming on the left, so I waited. When the road was clear, I rolled out into the street.

Bang! Crash!

I screamed and braked again. Two of the neighbor's metal trash cans went rolling down the street. Lester swore under his breath, got out and returned them, waved to the neighbors, and got back in. Now I was crosswise in the road, and a car was coming in each direction.

"Lester!" I screamed again.

"Al, will you please quit screaming?" he said. "Put the car in drive. Then slowly—*slowly*—turn the wheel and get out of the way of that BMW."

In the rearview mirror I could see the car behind me inching forward. I pushed the gearshift to *D* and moved the car over to the right side of the road so the car facing me could get by. As soon as it had passed, the car behind me gunned its motor and went tearing around us.

"Did I dent anything?" I asked in a shaky voice.

"No. The bumper hit the cans. Now move."

"I'm scared," I said.

"Be grateful," Les told me. "When I was learning to drive, we had a manual transmission. You've got power brakes, power steering, automatic transmission. . . . Piece of cake!"

Lester had me drive to the empty parking lot at the grade school and made me practice pulling in and out of parking spaces. I did so well after a half hour that he tried to teach me to parallel park behind a small bulldozer that was parked at one end.

"Jeez! Stop!" he yelled at one point. "Al, you came within an inch of scraping the side."

I was near tears. "I'm not ready for this, Lester!" I said.

"Okay, okay, we'll save that for another time. Let's go back through the neighborhood and call it a day," he said.

"I'm sorry," I murmured.

"For what?"

"For laughing at you when *you* were learning to drive," I sniffled. "I'm really sorry."

"Well, you should be," he said.

I steered in the direction Les was pointing and turned left. "I'm sorry I clapped and carried on when you were trying to park and knocked over that bucket with the broom in it," I said.

"Okay," said Lester.

"I'm sorry I made so much noise in the backseat and—"

"Al! You just went through a red light!" Lester yelled. "Watch what you're doing!"

"You said I could make a right turn on red, Lester!" I howled.

"Not when another car's coming, you can't! I'd like to live long enough to raise a family, you know."

He seemed even more relieved than I was when we reached our street and I finally made it up the driveway.

"So if you live long enough to raise a family, will it be with Tracy?" I asked, taking a chance on being nosy.

"Why? Has Dad said anything to you about her?" he wanted to know.

"He said you have a good head on your shoulders."

He grinned. "I do. And so does she."

• • •

At the "Our Whole Lives" class the next morning we had our infamous "putting a condom on a banana" lesson. It was too funny to be embarrassing. For some reason, the guys seemed more embarrassed than the girls, but we were all good sports about doing it. Gayle and Bert were good sports about answering our questions too, questions like, "What happens if a condom comes off inside a woman?"

"So what *do* you do?" Liz asked on the bus the next morning when I was explaining all this to her and Pamela.

"It doesn't usually happen, but you can fish it out with your fingers if you have to. Or the man could do it for you. It's not like you're some endless cave."

Liz cringed.

"So what else did they ask?" Pamela wanted to know.

I grinned. "Whether condoms make a noise if they pop. We spent part of the class just blowing them up like balloons, then holding them closed and popping them."

"I don't understand your church," said Liz. "When I go to mass, everything I touch is revered—a rosary, a prayer book, a candle. . . ."

I thought about that some. "I guess you could say we revere life," I told her, "and so do you. Sex is part of life, so my church isn't so different, really."

That got me thinking some more about my feature article on what students worry about. I was quite sure no one at school would confess any worries about condoms or possibly even religion, but I wondered if even my best friends would level with me.

So on Monday I buttonholed as many strangers as I could—kids in the cafeteria, in the gym, at their lockers, in the halls—and told them what I was working on. I said I didn't want their names, because we weren't using any in the article, but I wanted to know the things they worried about most.

Some kids, of course, said they never worried at all.

"What? Me worry?" one guy said, trying to imitate the face on those old collector's copies of *Mad* magazine.

But a surprising number gave me straight answers, and when I had collected all I could, I wrote down the different responses. Then I put a check mark beside each response every time a student named it as a worry. I arranged the list so that the worry with the most check marks was number one, the worry with the least was number eleven. Here's what I got:

1. Death and dying, me or someone I love
2. Being accepted by my friends

3. Grades and getting into college
4. Pain, surgery, hospitals, needles, etc.
5. The way I look
6. Finding the right person to marry
7. Being raped or kidnapped
8. Car wrecks
9. Change
10. Getting pregnant or a sexually transmitted disease
11. War or a terrorist attack

I showed the list to Sam the next day. "What do you think?" I said.

"Numbers one, two, six, and eight, yeah," he answered. "Numbers four, five, seven, and ten, never."

"What's the *worst* thing you can imagine?" I asked.

"Something happening to Mom. It's the 'only-child syndrome,' I guess," he said. "What about you?"

"It's already happened," I told him. "I already lost mine."

Elizabeth's very careful when she gets dressed about what goes with what. "Do these colors clash?" she asks us. "Can I wear a print with this belt?" "Should I tuck this in or wear it out?" "Buttoned or unbuttoned?"

So when we were figuring out what to pack for

New York, Liz brought over an armload of clothes, dumped them on my bed, and we began. "Which goes best with these pants?" she asked, holding up two sweaters. "This one or that one?"

I'd been mulling over the stuff in my own suitcase. I'd kept it open on my desk, putting things in or taking stuff out for several days in hopes that by the time we left on Friday, the clouds would part and a voice from heaven would tell me what to leave behind.

"Do you figure it will be cold enough for sweaters?" I asked. So far April had been especially mild, with everything blooming early.

"It's always colder in New York than you think," said Elizabeth.

I wouldn't know. I was studying the two sweaters she was holding when the cell phone in my backpack went off. *Not Sam,* I hoped. I really wanted to do most of my packing now and had set aside the whole evening for it. I was afraid he might want to come over.

"The boyfriend?" Liz asked. "Don't answer."

But I couldn't do that. I reached down on the floor for my backpack and checked the number. It was Pamela.

"Where are you?" she asked, almost spitting out the words. "Are you home?"

"Yes," I said, puzzled. "And Liz is here."

"I'm coming over," Pamela said, and the phone went dead.

I looked at Liz. "It was Pamela. What did I *do*? She sounds furious about something."

"I could hear her clear over here," said Liz. "I guess we'll soon find out."

Mentally going over everything I'd said to Pamela in the past couple of days, I tried to remember anything that might have set her off. Anything she might have taken as a snub. Anything she'd told me in private that I might have somehow passed along to someone else.

Pamela must have run all the way over because she got there sooner than we expected. It seemed like only a minute had passed before I heard the doorbell ring and, only seconds after that, the incessant knocking.

Sylvia's footsteps sounded on the floor below, hurrying to answer. Then Pamela's footsteps running up the stairs. She didn't even say hello to Sylvia.

When Pamela burst into my bedroom, I could tell she had been crying, but she looked as though she could tear the place apart with her teeth. I was almost afraid to get too close.

"What's the matter?" I asked.

"Mom!" she cried, her voice shaking with rage. "She's going to New York!"

"What?" I said.

Liz didn't get it. "She's moving to New York?"

"She's going *with* us!" Pamela shrieked. "She called the school and volunteered to go as one of the chaperones. I just found out!"

16

We're Off!

We could only stare in disbelief.

"How did she even know about the trip?" I asked.

"I guess she came over to the school and picked up a newspaper. She signed up a month ago and just told me! And she told the office that I could room with her, so they've put someone else in with you!" Pamela was practically shouting.

"And she didn't even *ask* you first?" I questioned.

"No!" Pamela cried. "I *hate* her! I just hate her! And I won't room with her. I *won't!*"

"Well, you can still sleep in our room!" Elizabeth said defiantly. "We'll sleep three in a bed or make a place for you on the floor if we have to."

"Yes!" I said, feeling angry at Mrs. Jones too. We'd had this all planned! "It doesn't matter what she told the school, you don't have to room with her. We asked first! Just don't!"

"I won't!" said Pamela. "I'm not even going to talk to her. As far as I'm concerned, I don't even know her. When she called and told me, I hung up on her." Pamela sat down to calm herself.

We were quiet for a minute or two. I knew exactly how Pamela felt—Dad signing me up for those church classes without asking me first. Except I didn't hate him.

"It's not like she'll be all alone if you don't room with her," said Liz, relenting a little. "She'll have other parents to talk to."

"Who cares?" said Pamela. "Did she care that *I* was alone after she left us—Dad and me?"

We sat there trying to make sense of it.

"Do you think she's checking up on you? Afraid of what you might do?" I asked, aware that Mrs. Jones didn't know the half of it.

"If she's so worried about what I might do in New York, why didn't she worry about what I might have been doing the two years I didn't have a mother at all? No, she sees it as a chance to ruin a good thing, that's what!"

Strangely, I felt a pang of sympathy for Mrs. Jones. "Maybe she's just trying to get close to you," I said.

"The only way I'll feel closer to her is if we stay ten miles apart," said Pamela. Her breathing began to slow and her shoulders slumped.

"What did your dad say about it?" Liz asked her.

"He says that just shows how impulsive she is. She does things on the spur of the moment."

"How *is* your dad, Pamela?" I asked. "Is he still dating that nurse?"

"No, not for a while." Pamela shook her head. "You know what I think? Crazy as it sounds, in some way I think he still loves her. And the only way they can seem to get close is to scream and yell at each other. I mean, is it possible that it's like . . . like a substitute for sex or something? All that emotion and fighting over the phone?"

"This is deep, deep stuff," said Liz. "They should see a marriage counselor."

"I *mean* it!" said Pamela. "It's like they get off on fighting with each other. Like they get some kind of high from all that screaming."

It was possible, I thought. We sat there shaking our heads. Finally Liz held up the two sweaters again. "This one . . . or that one?" she asked Pamela.

Pamela looked them over. "Ditch them both and bring something with a plunging neckline, Liz. We are going to *party,* and Mom's going to be sorry she ever came," she said.

There was a short assembly the day before our trip, for everyone going to New York. Mr. Corona, one of the history teachers, was handing out printouts of rules and regulations.

"Turn to page two," he was saying, "and check to see if we've signed you up for your choice of activity Saturday night. Everyone turn to page two. . . ."

Pamela had cramps, so she skipped the meeting, but the rest of us were there.

"Hi, roommate," Molly said when she sat down beside me next to the aisle.

"What?" I said.

"I just found out I'm rooming with you in New York," she said, her big blue eyes smiling. "You and Gwen and Liz."

"Terrific!" I said. "We wondered who the fourth girl would be!" Then I told her about Pam and her mom.

"We'll squeeze Pamela in with us, don't worry," said Molly. "It won't be the first time I've slept on the floor."

Ron and Faith came in and sat down in the row behind us. They had obviously been arguing. Molly rolled her eyes at me. Every so often we got snatches of their conversation behind us.

". . . thought I'd made that clear," Ron was saying.

". . . too late to get my deposit back, and Mom says I have to go." Faith sounded on the verge of tears.

More whispers.

Ron: ". . . either we both go or we both stay."

Faith: ". . . can't help it, Ron!"

Ron: "You want to be with Harry. Admit it!"

The art teacher in the audience, who was also chaperoning, turned around to see who was talking, and for a while neither Faith nor Ron said anything. Then the whispers started again.

Faith: ". . . but you told me you were going!"

Ron: "Well, I'm telling you now I'm not. I couldn't get the money. What I think is that you *want* to go without me."

"Ron!"

More whispers. Whimpers. Mutterings. Protests. . . .

". . . so you've got to choose." Ron was getting up.

"Ron!" Faith said again.

"Choose," he said again, and went out.

All I could hear after that was Faith's quiet crying and the drone of Mr. Corona's voice down in front.

We fully expected Faith to back out of the trip and were surprised to see her get out of her mom's car early Friday morning and board one of the buses to New York.

Mrs. Jones had been assigned to the other bus,

we found out upon asking, so we promptly followed Faith to bus number two, where she sat, tear-streaked, by a window.

Ron stood outside in the parking lot, hands in his pockets, staring without expression up at her window. Faith's mom was standing outside *her* car, arms folded, making sure, I guess, that Faith didn't get off the bus.

"She hates him!" Faith said to me, weeping. "Both my parents do. They'd be happy if I never saw Ron again."

They're not the only ones, I thought.

Faith dabbed at her eyes with a tissue. "He's going to be so lonely here by himself all weekend," she said, and her nose sounded clogged. "I told him I'd call three times a day, and he said not to bother. He's got this idea that I like Harry."

"Who doesn't?" said Molly. "But he's gay."

That was news to me. Harry, a senior this year, was one of the nicer guys in stage crew.

"I *told* Ron that, but he says Harry's gay till he gets me alone, and then I'll find out how hetero he really is."

"Look, Faith. You're going to New York with us, and you're going to have a good time," Molly told her. "Look around you! You're surrounded by friends!" Faith gave her a weak smile, and Molly squeezed her shoulder.

It was barely light out, but the bus was filling up fast. And here came Pamela's mother, looking for her. Seeing us sitting near the back, she smiled bravely and waved, then slowly maneuvered down the aisle toward us. She was holding a bag of something. Her smile looked unnatural, as though she had to hold it on to her face with her back teeth.

A group of noisy guys were trying to squeeze a carry-on bag on the luggage shelf, separating us from Mrs. Jones.

"Here, Pamela!" she called, trying to reach around them. "I made you girls some caramel corn for the trip."

There was Mrs. Jones, holding the bag. There we were, sitting like deaf-mutes. It was too embarrassing. I finally reached around the boys and took the bag. "Thanks," I said.

"See you in New York!" she chirped, her voice wavering a little as she studied her daughter. Then she turned and went back up the aisle.

Liz looked at Pamela staring out the window. Then she looked at Faith, silently weeping at another. "Some party!" she said to me, and we gave each other a sad smile.

I think we were all relieved when the buses finally started up and rolled away from the school. But suddenly I jerked to attention and looked around. "Where's Sam?" I said. I stood up and tried to see who all was on our bus. "Has anyone seen Sam Mayer?" I called out.

Justin, sitting toward the middle with Jill, turned around and said, "He came running out of the building just before we started up, and one of the teachers waved him toward the other bus."

"Well, *that* stinks!" said Liz.

I was disappointed at first but decided Sam and I could ride together on the bus back. We wouldn't be leaving New York until five Sunday afternoon and wouldn't get back to the school till around ten. It would be a lot more fun going on a long bus ride with a boyfriend after dark, I figured. A *lot* more fun.

Pamela began to perk up now that her mom was on the other bus. Brian and some of the guys we knew were sitting behind us. Brian had a brochure about a raunchy strip show in New York, and he and the guys were looking at it and laughing. Pamela kept asking to see it up close. Finally Brian dangled it over the seat in front of her face, and we got a quick glimpse. Pamela laughed and tried to grab the brochure away from him. Brian pulled it back.

Some of the girls down near the front started to sing, and then someone gave the driver a CD of the music the band had played at the Jack of

Hearts dance. As the music came over the sound system I thought about the way Sam had held me close to his chest that night, and I began to miss him.

Faith, too, was probably thinking of the dance and of Ron. She had a tissue wadded up in her hand. Her mom was right, I think, to insist that she come on the trip, Ron or no Ron. If Faith had been my daughter, I would have driven her to the school too and stood out there to be sure she didn't get off the bus. Maybe this would give Faith a chance to see that there was life without Ron. Maybe she would have such a good time in New York that things would never be the same again! Or . . . what if things were even worse for her once she got back?

17

The Big Apple

I figured New York couldn't be much different from Chicago, but . . . the people! All the *people*! We must have entered Manhattan over the lunch hour, because people were pouring out of buildings like ants, walking all spread out on the sidewalks.

Men were unloading racks of clothes off the backs of trucks, rolling them down the street into stores. Messengers in sleek biking outfits wove in and out of traffic. Women in jeans and boots, in silk coats and heels, were rushing down the avenues. There were people of every color, and everyone was in a hurry. Cabdrivers honking, policemen whistling, vendors calling, friends laughing . . .

As soon as I stepped off my bus, Sam was waiting. He grabbed and kissed me in front of my friends. We stood in line together in the Holiday

Inn. I couldn't tell if the manager was glad to see us or not. I'm sure he was glad to fill up his rooms. He just didn't want to fill them up with us, a high school history group from Silver Spring.

"I missed you," Sam whispered in my ear.

"We'll ride back together," I promised.

"It'll be a lot more fun than sitting with Tony Osler," said Sam. "He's not as pretty either."

Mrs. Jones looked like a fish out of water. Pamela was standing in line with Gwen and Molly and Liz, totally ignoring her mother. Mrs. Jones waited off to one side, smiling that smile that just looked too happy to be real. I tried not to look at them. It was too painful.

Mr. Corona stood with the clerk at the registration desk and called out the names for each room, handing out keys. In twos and threes and fours, people picked up their bags and headed for the elevators, and the line began to dwindle.

"Justin, Mark, Tim, and Sam," Mr. Corona called.

Sam kissed me again and went up to the desk for his key.

"Pamela Jones and Mrs. Jones," called Mr. Corona.

I saw Pamela tense up, her back rigid.

"That's us, Pam. Let's go, honey," her mom said. Pamela didn't move.

Elizabeth nudged her. "Go on. You have to sign in, but you don't have to stay there," she whispered.

Pamela walked stiffly up to the desk for her key, then over to the elevator, walking about six feet away from her mom.

"She looks like she's going to the gallows," said Gwen.

When Gwen and Liz and Molly and I got up to our room on the seventh floor, I ran over to the window to look at the New York skyline. I pulled back the drapes and found myself staring at the air-conditioning system on the roof of the building next door. There was only a small piece of sky farther on. I wheeled back around, disappointed, but Gwen and Molly broke into laughter.

"Welcome to New York!" Molly said. "What did you expect at student rates?"

Liz and I said we'd squeeze Pamela into our bed, so Molly and Gwen took the bed nearest the door. We dumped our bags wherever we found an empty space—nobody bothered with drawers— and we grabbed what we figured we'd need for the rest of the day.

We were supposed to meet back in the lobby at one, pick up a boxed lunch, then board the buses again for a trip to the Tenement Museum to see how early immigrants lived when they came to New York City.

It would be a full three days. Tomorrow, Ellis Island; tomorrow night, a play; Sunday, the Metropolitan Museum of Art and the UN, then the long trip home. Meals would be pretty much on the run, they'd told us.

We were just getting ready to leave the room when Pamela came dashing in.

"Where's your bag?" I asked.

She pointed to her backpack and dropped it in one corner. "I took a bunch of things out of my suitcase and stuffed them in here," she said. "So technically, I'm rooming with Mom, but I'm sleeping here."

"Is she mad?" asked Gwen.

"She doesn't know it yet," Pamela said. "She probably thinks I'm coming back!" She walked toward our window, her arms spread wide. "Bring on New York!" she said. Then she saw the air-conditioning units on the neighboring roof. "Well, at least you get a piece of sky from your window. All Mom and I can see is a wall."

Sort of a metaphor for the two of them, I thought.

Sam stayed glued to me on the ride to the Tenement Museum. We'd each chosen a different boxed lunch, and I didn't like my ham and cheese, so he fed me bites of his chicken salad.

"I make great chicken salad myself," he said. "I'm trying to learn to cook at least seven good things so that I can make something different every day of the week."

"You planning to do your own cooking in college?" I asked. "No dorm food for you, huh?"

He just smiled. "Maybe I'll cook for you sometime. I cook once a week for Mom and me."

"Yeah?"

"We took a class together in Chinese cooking. Now she wants me to go out for wrestling in my junior year."

"*Wrestling?*"

"Says it'll balance me out. You know, photography . . . cooking . . . wrestling . . ."

"What do *you* want to do?" I asked.

"You don't like wrestling? What would you suggest?"

"It's *your* life, Sam. Nobody else should decide that for you."

Mrs. Jones came down the aisle just then holding a large trash bag for our empty cartons. I hadn't realized until now that Pamela was on the other bus and wondered if this is the way it would be all weekend—Pamela waiting to see which bus her mom was on, then taking the other one.

The driver made a few detours to show us Rockefeller Center and the Empire State Building, then went on to 97 Orchard Street on the Lower East Side. When we got out, a tour director for the Tenement Museum divided us into groups of fifteen. She signaled me to go on in with the first group, but Sam wanted us to be together, so he held me back for the second group and Liz went in my place.

I think we were all impressed. The museum was an actual tenement building from 1863, and we got to see three of the tiny apartments that had been preserved and furnished, as nearly as possible, with the actual possessions of the families who had lived there. The guide told us their stories. The husband who found he could not provide for his family and, in disgrace and despair, simply disappeared. The mother who supported her family as a seamstress, turning dresses inside out or back to front to preserve them, as most of the women had only a dress for Sunday and an everyday dress, passed down from one family member to the next. The children who had no other place to play except the dimly lit stairs. . . .

None of us was prepared for just *how* small the rooms were—and so many people per room! Since each apartment stretched from front to back, only the room at the front had a window generally, and large openings were often cut in the walls between rooms so that light and air could travel from one to the other. A bedroom was scarcely big enough for a double bed, and there were, of course, no closets.

"Where did they put all their stuff?" Pamela asked in amazement.

The guide gave us a patient smile. "What stuff?" she asked. "All the possessions they owned could be stored beneath their beds."

I tried to imagine Liz and Pamela and me sleeping in one bed and storing all our stuff underneath. We wouldn't even be able to store all the stuff we'd brought for this trip, much less the things we had back home.

We asked about fire in the buildings. About sanitation. It was Gwen who asked the most questions about disease, and it was frightening to hear how easily measles and scarlet fever could spread from one tenement to the next.

Sam was running his hand up and down my back underneath my jacket. Then it inched its way above the waistband of my jeans and under my top. His fingers almost reached my bra in back. Then they stopped. It's hard to concentrate on immigrants when a guy's fingers are roaming around your back.

The buses took us to an Italian fast-food place for dinner, and then we had two choices for New York at night. We could walk with a group to Times Square or head in the other direction for a walk through Central Park, stopping to look at a landmark restaurant called Tavern on the Green.

Pamela, Liz, and I huddled in a restroom to talk it over.

"I heard someone say we'd be getting back to the hotel early tonight because we have to be up early tomorrow," Pamela said. "So let's not break away till we've checked in back at the hotel later. If we ditch too early, they'll send us home."

"Let's see if we can get Gwen to go with us," I said. "Molly, too."

"All right. But keep it tight. We don't want it to get around," said Pamela.

We had to sign up early for the evening activity. No one had the option of staying back at the hotel. I'd seen the silver ball descending at Times Square on New Year's Eve so many times on TV that this didn't much interest me. Besides, Sam wanted to do the walk through Central Park at night, so we signed up for that. The air was balmy for April—especially mild for New York, we'd been told—and it felt good to be out walking after a long day on the bus.

Some of the stage crew were in our group—Harry and Faith and Chris. Sam and I hung back at the end, our arms around each other, kissing when we got the chance. I liked listening to the soft *clop-clop* of horses' hooves as carriages passed us, pulled by horses wearing hats decorated with flowers.

Maybe it was the couples cuddling under warm blankets in the carriages that made me want to be closer to Sam. Some of the tops were up on the carriages, so the couples were barely visible and you could only imagine what was going on under that flimsy top. Under the *blanket,* maybe!

Even before we got to the restaurant, we could see why Tavern on the Green was so popular. Sitting on the western edge of Central Park, the trunks of its trees were decorated with hundreds of tiny lights. Lanterns hung from the highest branches to the lowest, so you felt you were approaching a fairyland. It was booked solid for the evening, and all we could do was walk around outside, where the bushes had been sculpted into birds and animals. The lights, the breeze on our faces, Sam's arm around me . . . I almost felt guilty for planning the rest of the evening without including Sam.

We followed a lighted path down into the park for a short walk, all staying together in one group. Past the night joggers, the dog walkers, the police officers on horseback, the homeless. Once, stopping at a large outcropping of rock, Sam backed me up against it and pressed against me as we kissed. My whole body seemed to want him. I guess this is how Gwen felt when she let Legs, her old boyfriend, do IT. How Liz felt when she let Ross touch her. How we were *supposed* to feel when we were making out. Too bad that wasn't on the agenda.

When we got up to the street again, carriages were lined up along the curb, waiting for new passengers. The drivers, in top hats, called out friendly greetings, and one of them asked Faith if she wanted to feed his horse a sugar cube.

"If the horse won't take it, you can feed it to me," he joked, flirting with her, and when Faith smiled, her teeth shone pure white in the moonlight. *That girl should smile more often,* I thought. She should have more to smile about. Funny how you focus on teeth when your own have braces.

I liked to see the way she blossomed when Ron wasn't around. She had changed from black clothes to white, as she usually did in summer, so she looked more like a bride than a widow. I think she buys vintage clothes at thrift shops, and she was wearing a long rayon dress with a matching stole and little lace-up granny boots.

The driver, a young man around twenty, put a sugar cube in the palm of Faith's hand and kept hold of her hand when she offered it to the horse.

The big brown and white animal with the chest-nut eyes swooped its head down toward her, noiselessly grazing her palm, took the sugar, then sniffed at her hand once more.

"Oh!" she cried, stroking its long muzzle.

"Here!" Chris said, and produced an apple from a jacket pocket.

"He'll eat it? The whole thing?" Faith asked the driver.

"Well, not unless you peel it first," the driver teased, and we all laughed.

Faith held the apple out and watched the horse take it and stand chewing, little bits of pulp and seeds dropping from its mouth.

"Oh, I love you," Faith whispered to the horse, and it rewarded her with a quick buss on the side of her head.

"I'm so glad she came on this trip," I told Sam.

18

Breaking Out

We got back to the hotel about nine thirty, and the teachers reminded us that there would be a "lockup" of all rooms at ten o'clock.

"I think it's all talk," said Elizabeth. "How can they possibly do it? Lock us in from the outside?"

"I think it just means they check us off at ten, and we're on the honor system after that," said Gwen.

"No way," said Pamela. "Can you imagine the guys staying in their room all night? *Brian?*"

Molly agreed. "But they did say 'lockup,' not 'check up.'"

"Maybe there's a guard at all the exit doors taking names," I suggested.

"That's not the problem, Alice," said Molly. "What if nobody wants to go out? What if all a guy wants to do is get in a girl's room?"

I immediately thought of Sam.

"Does your mother know where you are, Pamela?" asked Gwen. "Somebody better tell her."

"I left her a note," said Pamela. "I said that since she decided to come along as a chaperone without asking me if it was okay, I decided to room with you guys without asking her if it was okay."

"Won't she tell someone?" asked Molly.

"No. Can you imagine her telling the teachers that her own daughter doesn't want to stay in the same room with her?"

I studied Pamela for a moment. "Are you ever going to forgive her?" I asked.

Pamela just tossed her head, and I could tell it wasn't a topic she wanted to discuss. Instead, she told Gwen and Molly about the clubs we were going to look up once we found a way to get out. "You want to be in on it?" she asked.

"Sure!" said Gwen.

"I'd better not," said Molly. "I'm trying to get into Oberlin next year. I'd be upset if anything went on my record."

It wasn't long before we found out what "lockup" meant. Karen and Jill called us from another room. "They came and put tape on the door!" Karen cried. "Can you believe it?"

"Tape?" I said. "They think tape is going to keep us in?"

"No, but they said they'll be making rounds

throughout the night, and if anyone's tape is disturbed, they'll know somebody went in after lockup," she answered.

Maybe teachers were smarter than we thought.

Just then we heard tapping on the door next to ours.

"Hide Pamela!" Gwen instructed us. "They'll be here next!"

Pamela slid off the bed and tried to crawl under it, but the space was too narrow.

"The closet!" Liz whispered frantically, and we got her in the closet and threw our backpacks in on top of her. A couple of minutes later one of the chaperones knocked on the door. A pleasant-faced woman with little black-framed glasses stepped inside, holding a list.

"Hi, girls," she said. "This is . . . 714, right? Am I looking at Gwen, Alice, Elizabeth, and Molly?"

"Yep," we said.

She looked around. "Everything okay? Nobody needs any ice or anything? Once I tape the door, kiddos, you're in for the night. Unless there's an emergency, of course."

"We're fine," said Elizabeth.

"Okay. Have a good sleep. Breakfast at seven. There will be cereal and muffins in the hospitality suite on the sixth floor."

"Good night," we chorused as she went back out and closed the door after her.

Pamela came out of the closet.

"Now what?" I said.

"I guess that about cooks it for us, doesn't it?" said Liz disappointedly. "They've put us all on the sixth and seventh floors. Even if we could open the window, we couldn't crawl out."

"I'll think of something!" said Pamela. "Back to the robes and the smoke, maybe."

Gwen turned on the TV, and what did we get? Previews for adult entertainment. "See what we're missing?" she joked.

We flipped channels while Pamela paced. Molly got ready for bed, but—ever the optimists—we didn't. Ten fifteen became ten thirty. Then the phone rang. I reached over and picked it up.

"Room 714?" came a pleasant-sounding male voice.

"Yes," I said.

"There's a delivery down at the front desk. You'll need three or four girls to pick it up."

"What?" I said. "What is it?"

"I . . . can't quite tell," said the voice.

"We can't leave the room. You'll have to deliver it," I said.

"You have permission to come down and get this," the man said. "But you might want to check the hallway before you come down in case there's a misunderstanding."

"Well . . . all right," I said, and put the phone down.

"Who was it?" asked Pamela.

"The front desk!" I said, puzzled. "We're supposed to go down and pick up a delivery. He said it would take three or four girls to carry it."

"*What?* What is it?" asked Elizabeth.

"He said he couldn't tell. I'll bet it's just cumbersome or something. A huge order of balloons, maybe."

"How did he know we were all girls in this room?"

"It's the way we're registered," I said. "C'mon. Let's all go."

Molly was already in her pajamas. "He said three or four girls. You don't need me. I'm pooped."

Gwen was skeptical. "I don't trust this," she said. "Who did he say he was?"

"He didn't. He just said, 'Room 714?'"

"I knew it!" said Gwen. "The front desk wouldn't repeat the number of the room they just called! They can tell from their computerized phones what room they're talking to."

"Oh, Gwen, you're paranoid," said Pamela, excitedly pulling on her shoes. "All we're doing is going down to the lobby. We're not meeting someone out in an alley or anything. What can happen? There are four of us, and we've got a perfect excuse. If Mr. Corona stops us, we'll tell him the front desk called and said there was a delivery."

"Well, retape the door after you go out," said Molly. "We can't have somebody knocking on the door, wondering where you are."

I peeked out the peephole to be sure there wasn't a sleazy man in a trench coat waiting to push into the room as soon as the door was open. The corridor appeared to be clear.

I turned the handle and slowly inched the door open a crack. I heard the adhesive give and, looking up, saw a wide piece of duct tape hanging loose near the top of the doorway.

The four of us went out and carefully pressed the tape back in place. Then we walked quickly down the hall to the elevator, pushed the button, and got on.

When we got to the lobby and stepped out, Brian and Tony Osler and a guy I'd seen around school, a senior, I think, were waiting for us.

"Room 714?" said the senior, grinning, and I recognized the voice on the phone.

I started to laugh, but the guys grabbed our arms and ushered us across the lobby to a side entrance, away from the front desk.

"What's going on?" asked Liz, as if we didn't know.

"Party time!" Brian sang as we stepped outside.

"Hey! How are we supposed to get back in our rooms?" Gwen asked.

"No problemo! I'll follow you up and retape your door," Tony said.

"Then how will *you* retape yours?" I asked.

"I'll tip a bellhop," said Tony. "In fact"—he paused and grinned—"it's all arranged."

"Absolutely brilliant!" said Pamela.

More than that, the guys had brought sweatshirts for us since we had come down without jackets, so we put them on and followed them down the sidewalk.

"I'm Hugh," the senior said. He had dark curly hair, a jacket thrown over one shoulder, a huge chest and broad shoulders. Pamela hardly took her eyes off him. He laughed at the way we looked in their oversized sweatshirts, my maroon and gold Terps shirt coming halfway down my thighs. I laughed too, at the sight of us, at the way things were working out, at being outside in New York on a mild April night with my three best friends and three guys. I mean, this was even better than we thought!

"So where are we going?" I asked.

"First the subway," said Hugh. "Then we'll try a couple places, see if we can get in."

If Sam could see me now, I thought, he'd freak out.

I refused to even *think* what Dad or Les would say.

We went down a flight of concrete steps to the subway, and Hugh bought some MetroCards. Once on the train Gwen asked, "Where did you learn so much about New York?"

"Used to live here," Hugh said. "I know some bars over by NYU. My brother used to go there, so he told me some good places." He smiled at Gwen and nodded toward her sweatshirt. "You're a natural," he said. NYU was on the front. He was probably right; Gwen could have passed for a freshman.

The subway cars rattled along the track, and we swayed this way and that, our upper bodies leaning against each other as the train tipped from left to right. We were seated three on one side, facing the three on the other, and Pamela was odd man out. So she sat down on Hugh's lap rather than sit on a seat by herself. As the car shook she wiggled around with a slightly exaggerated movement. "Lap dancing," she said, and the guys laughed.

Hardly anyone stares at you in New York, even on the subway. In our car there were two Latino women talking with each other, an elderly man with his eyes half closed, a student reading a textbook, a student reading a newspaper. . . . You get the feeling after a while that you could get on the subway stark naked and people would just glance your way and go on reading.

At the NYU stop we got off and, after a couple of blocks, turned onto a street alive with students. Some were sitting at outdoor tables eating, talking, kissing, collars turned up. Others were waiting in lines to get in a movie or a club, and still others were sitting on the stone steps of buildings, chatting, smoking. . . .

I don't know why this always happens to me, but I realized I had to pee. Bad. If I'd known we were going to be out with the guys, I would have gone before we left, but now there was a sense of urgency that told me every step I took was a potential disaster.

"Hey," I said. "Anybody else need a restroom?"

Hugh, walking up ahead with Pamela and Tony, turned around. "We've only got about six more blocks. Can you wait?"

I gave him an agonized look. "Maybe not. I didn't know I'd be going anywhere tonight."

We all stopped, and Hugh glanced about. "Most places won't let you use the restroom unless you're a paying customer, but if you're cute and threaten to pee on their floor . . ." He nodded toward a club just ahead of us. "Go throw yourself on the mercy of the bouncer," he said.

"I'll go with you," said Elizabeth.

We stepped inside, and there were about a dozen people waiting for tables.

"Excuse me," I said, gently pushing past them. "Excuse me . . . excuse me . . ."

They gave us cold stares, and one man wasn't going to move till Liz said, "This is an emergency. She means it."

It was dark inside, the music loud and the floor plan confusing. I looked around to see if I could spot any door that looked like a restroom.

Suddenly a man stepped out of the shadows and confronted us. "Reservation?" he said.

I winced. "I'm not trying to get in your club. I just really, *really* have to use the restroom," I said.

"Sorry. Customers only."

"It's an emergency," I said.

"She means it too!" said Elizabeth again. "She'll do it right here on the floor."

The man gave us a disgusted look, but he didn't want to take the chance. He nodded toward the back of the room.

Elizabeth and I zigzagged our way through the tables till we got to the restroom door. Inside were two tiny stalls. I took one, Liz the other.

"Oh, man, what a relief!" I said.

"You sound like a cloudburst," said Liz on the other side of the partition.

I was about to flush when I heard someone come in. A man was humming to himself—humming and singing the words to a song.

"Oh, great!" I heard Liz say.

It was a unisex bathroom, but there was no lock on the door, only the stalls. The man seemed to be waiting there at the sink, singing to himself. Liz flushed, I flushed, and we both stepped out at the same time to see a tall woman in a black low-cut dress, fooling with her hair at the mirror. She looked at us and smiled. No, she looked at us and laughed at the way we were staring at her, and then she went in one of the stalls. We realized then that she was a he.

Wordlessly, we washed our hands and walked back through the club, past the bar, and on outside, where Pamela was tap-dancing on the sidewalk and Gwen was waiting, hands in her pockets, talking with the guys.

Elizabeth and I both let out whoops at once, covering our mouths with our hands.

"Okay, what did you see?" said Hugh, laughing.

"A man in the women's restroom. No, a unisex restroom," Liz said. "I mean a man in a woman's dress!"

Hugh laughed. "That's what that club is known for—transgendered performers. It was probably one of the singers."

I tried to be cool about it. About everything that was going on around me. If Carol were here, I thought, my twenty-something cousin back in

Chicago, this is exactly the type of thing we'd be doing. She loves exploring too.

Music was blaring out of another club down the street, and as we passed, Tony came up behind me, took my wrists in both hands, and, holding my arms out at the sides, danced me past the open door in time to the music. I was having a ball.

We reached the place Hugh had in mind. It was half bar, half restaurant, and obviously a place where students hung out.

"We're officially here for the food, okay?" he said. "But sometimes . . . if we're lucky . . ."

We followed him to a counter at the back, where they were selling sandwiches and nachos and cheese fries. A group in one corner got up to leave, and Tony grabbed their table. We confiscated empty chairs here and there until we had seven crowded around it.

"What do you want to drink?" asked Hugh.

"We didn't bring any money," I said. "I'm just along for the ride."

He smiled. "It's on me."

"Diet Pepsi," I said.

He took orders all around, and he and Tony and Brian went to the counter and placed our order. They came back with the sodas and huge orders of nachos and cheese fries. Hugh kept looking around the room while we ate, fingers tapping the table in time to the music, and then he said, "Hey!"

He turned back to me again. "What would you *really* like to drink, if you could?"

I tried to remember what we'd seen on those reruns of *Sex and the City*. "A Cosmopolitan?" I answered.

"Yeah," said Liz. "Me too."

He turned to Pamela and Gwen.

"Mojito for me," said Gwen, and Pamela seconded the order.

Hugh got up and walked over to a nearby table.

"Hey, Hugh!" an older guy said, and got up to shake his hand. "How's it going? How's your brother?"

They stood there talking awhile, and the older guy glanced at our table, then talked some more. Finally he smiled and gave a little nod, and Hugh came back.

"Just be cool," he said.

I didn't know how else to be cool except to sit there and do what I was doing anyway, which was listening to a band called Two-Face Fever, which wasn't very good. A few minutes went by. Then Hugh and Tony casually stood up and went to the friend's table again. This time they came back with three beers and two cocktails—one pink, the other a sort of greenish white.

"There were only five at that table, so that's all they could order without making the bartender suspicious," Hugh told us.

"It's okay," said Liz. "We'll share." Half a Cosmo was better than none at all.

Each of us—Gwen, Pamela, Liz, and I—had a couple sips of each. The Cosmo, with vodka and cranberry juice, Pamela thought, was stronger, but the Mojito was prettier, with mint leaves floating on top and a sweet sugary taste. I couldn't believe I was sitting in a bar in New York City, drinking a Cosmo—well, part of a Cosmo, anyway—with my friends. It was sort of like I belonged here. Like I did this every week! When the guy at the other table and his friends got up to leave, they glanced our way and smiled.

Any minute I figured somebody would come by and kick us out. They did, in a way. When Brian went back to the counter for another order of cheese fries, the bartender told him that when we finished the nachos, we had to give up our table. They don't miss very much, I guess. You can't try anything they haven't seen before.

"Go slow," Hugh urged us. "If they're still doing it, maybe we can stick around long enough to see some of the Friday Night Underwear Party."

"What?" said Liz.

He just smiled.

No one paid much attention to the band when the underwear party got going. We noticed that the place was getting more and more crowded, people pressing up against our chairs in back. But when the first customer stood up and slipped off his jeans, Elizabeth looked at me in horror.

"We don't have to do this, do we?" she asked.

"Sure, babe. Why do you think we brought you?" said Hugh.

"What?" said Gwen.

They were kidding, of course. The first customer went up on the flimsy stage and paraded across, with lots of whistles and applause and a drumroll from the band.

"Number one!" yelled the emcee, "Bill from Brooklyn!" We all cheered some more.

There were nine contestants in all, most of them a little boozy, two of them female, which surprised us. The girls weren't exactly like strippers, though—their underwear was more the cotton collegiate type—but they were bikini style, and the girls had nice bodies, so all the guys whistled and clapped. We didn't get to see the last four because the bartender came over and told us we were out. We left just as "Steve from New Jersey" was going across the stage.

"Darn!" said Elizabeth when we got outside. "Just when it was getting good!"

It was after one o'clock, and I didn't even want to think about trying to get back in our room. I didn't want to think about Sam or school or exams or braces. I had a little Cosmo in me, a little Mojito, and Gwen and Liz had their arms around each other as we walked back to the subway, singing theme songs from various TV shows and making us guess what they were.

When we got back to the hotel, Hugh made us wait outside till he saw the bellhop cross the lobby. He was doubling as clerk and bellhop this time of night. He went over to the elevator and gave us the sign when the door was open. Quiet as mice, we slipped in, jaws clenched to keep from laughing at the way Tony was imitating Mr. Corona giving instructions on the bus.

When we got to the seventh floor, Hugh looked out and gave the all-clear sign. Then suddenly he shoved us back in the elevator again as a door opened far down the hall. We pushed the button for the eleventh floor, rode up, then back, and this time when we stepped out on our floor, the hall was empty. Silently, we moved along till we came to our room.

Gwen slowly removed the duct tape from the door, and I slipped my key card in the slot. When I got the green light, I opened the door, and the four of us went inside, the guys acting like they were going to come in too, silently clowning around till we turned them out. I shut the door and could hear the soft swipe of a hand pressing the duct tape back on the door again. Through the peephole, I saw them disappear down the hall.

Molly rolled over and squinted when the bathroom light came on. "You guys have a good time?" she asked sleepily.

"It was great!" I said. "I wish you'd come with us, Molly. Brian and Tony and a senior named Hugh met us in the lobby. It was Hugh who called, and we went to a bar over near NYU. It was so much fun!"

She smiled. "When you didn't come back, I figured it was something like that."

"Did anything happen?" asked Pamela.

"One of the parent chaperones called to ask if Jill was in our room, and I had to tell her no," Molly said. "But no one asked about you."

I could hardly believe we'd gotten away with it. We had finally done something wild and crazy, and nobody got drunk, nobody got pregnant, nobody got stoned, nobody was drinking and driving.

We fell into bed, Liz and Pamela and I squeezed in together, but if any of us turned over in the night, we didn't know it.

In the morning when we got up, Liz found a

printed notice under our door. It said that tonight there would be a teacher or parent volunteer stationed out in the hall of the sixth and seventh floors all night and that any student caught leaving his or her room after lockup would not only be sent home, but suspended from school as well.

"Do you think they know?" Liz asked.

"Well, nobody called," said Molly.

"Maybe it was Jill they caught," mused Gwen.

"Or maybe somebody told on us after we got back," said Pamela.

We prepared ourselves for a lecture once we got downstairs.

19

Pamela . . . Again

Liz was in the bathroom, so I decided to pull on my jeans and sweatshirt, go down to the hospitality suite, and bring our breakfasts upstairs so we could eat while we dressed and save a little time. Because of my braces, I like to be able to brush after I eat. I hate to find out three hours later that there's a piece of lettuce caught in a wire.

I picked up my room key and opened the door. There stood Sam, leaning against the opposite wall, waiting for me. *Uh-oh,* I thought. *He's heard.* I hadn't even combed my hair! I hadn't washed my face or rinsed out my mouth.

"Sam!" I said, embarrassed, covering my mouth with one hand.

He grinned and came over to kiss me, but I wouldn't let him.

"I look horrible," I said.

"You're always beautiful to me," said Sam.

"So what are you? A stalker?" I kidded, walking quickly on down the hall, then the stairs to the sixth floor.

"I just wanted to say good morning," Sam said, and tried to kiss me again in the stairwell.

"I'm really in a hurry, Sam," I told him. "I wanted to bring breakfast to the other girls. I'll see you later, okay?"

"Okay," he said, disappointed.

In the hospitality suite I scooped up five plastic boxes and five cartons of milk and took them back to the room. We ate sitting on the edge of our beds, telling Molly more about our adventure of the night before. She laughed about Liz and me finding a transvestite in the unisex bathroom.

"I *wish* you'd come," I told her again.

"I would have, but I was just so tired. I'm beginning to feel I came to New York mostly to sleep," she said. "It's just nice to get away. What should we wear to Ellis Island, do you think? That ferry ride across the harbor could be chilly."

We got The Weather Channel on TV and it said breezy, so we opted for sweaters under our Windbreakers just in case.

"I'm going to look up my great-great-great-great-grandfather," said Molly. "When he came over from Ireland, he came through Ellis Island. You can look up a relative's name in the library there and find the name on a ship's passenger list. I'd like to make a copy of it and give it to Dad for his birthday."

That was such a wonderful idea, I wondered why I hadn't thought of it. Except I don't know my great-great-great-great-grandparents. In fact, I didn't even know the *grand*parents on my mother's side. They died before I was born. The only relatives I know, besides Aunt Sally and Uncle Milt and Carol, are Dad's two brothers, Howard and Harold, down in Tennessee, along with Grandpa McKinley, who usually doesn't remember me at all.

Sam was waiting again when we boarded the buses. We rode to Battery Park at the tip of Manhattan, where we waited in line again to board the ferry. There was a lot of gossip about who had gone out after lockup the night before. Evidently, we hadn't been the only ones, and if the other kids bribed the bellhop too, he must have made a mint.

"What time did *you* get to bed?" Sam asked me.

"Late," I told him.

And then we were on the ferry, and I was seeing the Statue of Liberty for the first time. She was so tall, I could hardly believe it. I tried to imagine what it must have been like for immigrants sailing into New York Harbor, looking at that magnificent lady lifting the torch.

At Ellis Island we were divided into groups of twenty and taken through the exhibits on the first floor. As we stopped at each one the guide told us about the long lines of immigrants waiting for the physical exam, which would either allow them to enter the country or would turn them away. I leaned back against Sam as we listened, his arms around my waist, fingers interlocked over my stomach. Sometimes, his face nuzzling my cheek, he'd work one hand inside my jacket in front, up under my shirt, then slide a finger slowly around under the waistband of my underwear, caressing my skin. It was deliciously sexy, and I was surprised to feel a wetness in my pants. Who would have thought that here on Ellis Island . . . ?

Mrs. Jones was assigned to our group this time, and when I wasn't concentrating on what the guide was telling us or what Sam's fingers were doing under my clothes, I stole a look at Mrs. Jones and noticed how nervous she seemed. It was as though one part of her body had to be in motion all the time—her feet or her fingers. . . . I guess I never knew her that well before, but one thing I'd never thought about her was that she was nervous.

There were sack lunches to eat outdoors, but I was still haunted by some of the photographs I'd seen in the exhibits. The eyes of a mother, holding a small child in her arms—looking terrified, it seemed—as she approached a doctor. Sometimes the children passed the exam but the mother didn't, our guide had said. Or the wife passed but not the husband. The anguish of their decision then—what to do?

"My great-great-great-great-great-grandparents came from Russia," Sam told some of us, sitting together on the grass. "They even changed their name so they could fit in better."

"Really?" Faith said. "What was it before?"

"Mayerschoff. I was named after my great-great-great-great-great-grandfather Samuel."

The April sun and the April breeze together made a terrific mix. It was chilly, but the sun was warm on our arms and legs. I looked over at another group to see Pamela lying on her back, her head in Hugh's lap. *Well,* that *was quick!* I thought. Jill was wrapped around Justin. I was leaning back against Sam, his legs on either side of me. Spring was definitely for couples, I thought, and I wondered if, back home, Patrick was going out with Marcie Bernardo this weekend. Wondered about Dad and Sylvia having the house to themselves for a change. About Les and Tracy and how their romance was going.

We toured the second floor after we ate, looking at the possessions immigrants brought with them:

a trunk, a bowl, a doll, a comb, medicine bottles, shoes. . . . I thought of the ones who went to tenements—whole families squeezing into two or three rooms. Sam told me about his great-great-great-great-great-grandmother Sophie and the locket she wore with two beautiful *S*'s engraved on it, for *Sophie* and her husband, *Samuel.* Maybe that's what made him such a romantic, I thought. Most girls would die for a guy who fawned over them the way Sam did me.

It was cloudy on the ferry going back and cold out on deck, so I sat snuggled up against him. It felt good to get back on the bus afterward. We were to eat dinner at another fast-food place, and then we had a choice between two off-Broadway productions: either a one-woman performance of Emily Dickinson or a one-man performance of George Gershwin. Sam and I signed up for Gershwin. I can't carry a tune—I couldn't sing a melody if I was put in front of a firing squad—but I can recognize *Rhapsody in Blue* when I hear it.

It should have been a romantic evening, and in a way it was. I'll have to admit that part of the attraction of getting close to a guy is not knowing just how far the two of you will go. Not knowing if the finger that caresses your back will slip up under your bra as though it got lost and didn't quite know where it was going, or whether, when you kiss and he presses up against you, you can feel him getting hard. It's sort of a game of "What Next?" that keeps you excited. Keeps you guessing.

But I also found myself vaguely irritated at times because he was always there. I didn't have a chance to miss him because he was never gone. When I got up to my room at last, I felt relief at just being with the girls. Gwen and Molly and Liz had chosen the Dickinson play and were talking about how good the actress had been.

I kicked off my shoes. "Where's Pamela?" I asked.

"She said she was going to get some more stuff from her mom's room," said Molly.

"Lockup's at midnight tonight," said Liz. "She's got twenty-five minutes."

"Do you really think a chaperone's going to sit out in the hall all night watching our doors?" I said. "I'll bet they check us once and that's it."

"I don't think so," said Molly. "I heard they're going to take shifts."

"So who wants to play cards?" said Liz.

"Naw," said Gwen. "What's on TV?"

"Not much," I said.

When a chaperone tapped on the door and did a room check, we passed with ease because Pamela, of course, wasn't on her list and wasn't in our room.

"You can sleep in a bit tomorrow, girls," she

said. "The museum doesn't open until nine thirty, but we're scheduling a jog through Central Park at seven. If you want to go, be down in the lobby in your running shoes."

"Right! Sure! Absolutely!" said Gwen, and we cheerfully wished the chaperone a good night.

But after the woman had closed the door and taped it, Liz said, "What are we going to do when Pamela comes back? Who's going to explain the loose tape on the door after she comes in?"

"That's her problem," said Gwen. "Maybe she'll find herself spending the night with her mom after all."

"It's been a good day, though," Molly told us. "Look." She showed us a printout of a ship's manifest with her great-great-great-great-grandfather's name on it. "Henry Franklin Brennan," she said. "My dad will really go for this!"

"My ancestors came over on a ship too, but I don't think you'll find their names on any passenger list," Gwen said.

That was a sobering thought.

"Don't you get angry sometimes?" Liz asked her.

"When I think about it," said Gwen. "But I don't think about it all the time. My friend Yolanda does, though. It's a crusade with her."

"How could you *not* think about it?" I asked. "How could you not be angry?"

"Because that was then and this is now," Gwen told us. "If you go around angry all the time, *you're* the one it hurts. I react to things that happen *today*. That's what I can fix. I can't fix the past."

We put on our flannel pajama bottoms and T-shirts and watched an old *Saturday Night Live* rerun. When a commercial came on, Liz said, "Do you think we should call Mrs. Jones's room and see if Pamela's there?"

"If she *is*, they're either asleep or arguing, and I wouldn't want to interrupt either one," I said. "And if she *isn't*, Mrs. Jones will flip out."

"Why wouldn't she have called us, though?" Gwen mused. "She knows we'd be wondering about her."

"Well, she got off the bus with me, and I saw her come inside, so we know she got that far," said Molly.

When the show was over, we turned off the TV. Liz was crawling under the covers when we heard tapping on the door. I ran to the peephole and jumped back when I saw Mr. Corona standing right outside, Pamela beside him!

"It's . . . it's *him*!" I whispered. "Corona!"

"Mr. Corona?" the others gasped.

"And Pamela!"

"O'm'God! Open the door!" said Molly.

I opened the door and heard the tape snap.

"Hi, guys!" she said, and looked directly at me, her eyebrows going up and down. "Mom said yes, I could spend our last night here with you." She winked.

"Well . . . great!" I said, as she stepped inside.

"Okay, this is it, girls," said Mr. Corona. "I'll tape up after you, but you're in now for the night."

"Thanks," said Pamela. "Good night, Mr. Corona."

I closed the door after him and stared at Pamela. "What's going *on*? How did you arrange *that*?"

"We thought you were with your mom," said Gwen.

"She hasn't called, has she?" Pamela asked, and without waiting for an answer, she went into the bathroom. We heard the water running in the sink. Heard Pamela brushing her teeth.

"How did you get Mr. Corona to do that?" I asked her again.

"Simple," said Pamela. "When I got off the elevator and saw him, I just walked right up to him and said Mom had given me permission to spend our last night with you guys and that I should let him know."

"So he thinks you came up from your mom's room?" Liz said.

"Easy as pie," said Pamela.

When she took off her clothes and got into bed,

Gwen sat facing her. "Okay, girl, where were you, then? We want scoop!"

"What do you mean?" Pamela said, acting the innocent.

"Molly said you went to your mom's room to get more stuff. Where is it?"

"Oh, I changed my mind. I was just hanging out with Hugh," Pamela said, a little too casually.

Elizabeth exchanged looks with Molly.

"Where?" asked Liz.

"I'm not sure, exactly. Hugh's room, I think. His buddies were watching TV." She giggled. "I *told* you I was going to have fun on this trip." She pulled the covers up under her chin as though that was all she had to say. But Gwen wouldn't let it go.

"So what happened?" she asked. "What'd you do?"

"Well, *you're* nosy, aren't you?" Pamela laughed.

"Yeah," said Gwen. "I am." She poked at her through the blanket. "C'mon. Give."

"Let's just say I was making somebody *reeeally* happy," said Pamela. "Okay?"

Not okay.

"Happy as in . . . sex?" asked Molly.

"You could say that," Pamela said coyly.

"You did . . . IT?" I said.

"Look! We were in his bathroom, okay? So I gave Hugh some head. Now are you satisfied?"

Gwen and I glanced at each other.

"A blow job?" Elizabeth asked.

"Yeah, Liz. You get a one hundred. A blow job is head is oral sex."

"But . . . why?" I asked. "You just met him."

For a second Pamela seemed thrown by the question. "Because he wanted it! It was fun! It was amazing to see how excited I could get him!"

I'll have to admit I was surprised. No, not surprised. I was shocked. I was also curious as anything. It was Liz, though, who asked the next question.

"Do you swallow it or what?"

We giggled, but I sure didn't know the answer.

"You can, but I didn't," Pamela told her.

Liz recoiled a little. "I can maybe see myself doing that with a guy I really loved, but . . . you hardly even know him, Pam!"

"I know him enough to know I like him. I think he's hot! And he's a senior."

"Yeah, but what are *you*? Just a body part? A head?" I asked.

And Gwen put in her two cents. "You're not a service station. Trust me. I should know what it's like when a guy just wants quick service. My old ex was a master at it."

"So are you going to burn me at the stake or what?" asked Pamela.

"I just want to make sure you know what you're doing," said Gwen. "You can get a venereal disease in your mouth, you know."

"Yeah, yeah, and I could get run over by a taxi or get hit by a meteorite," said Pamela. She closed her eyes.

"I just want you to be aware!" Gwen told her.

Pamela's eyes popped open again. "I'm aware! I'm aware! So I made a really cute guy happy tonight. It's no big deal." And then she turned to me. "Hugh and I really hit it off last night, Al, didn't you notice? Brian's history. I think Hugh really likes me. After tonight, in fact, I'm sure of it. What would you say if I said he was taking me to the prom?"

"Really? Did he ask?" Molly wanted to know.

"Not in so many words, but I think he's going to."

Wow. To tell the truth, I didn't know what to think. Was what Pamela felt that much different from the feelings I'd had at Ellis Island with Sam running his fingers under the waistband of my pants? Up under the band of my bra? My wanting him to go a little further? Touch me in other places, too?

"What are you thinking?" Pamela asked me after we'd turned out the light.

"Lots of things. Wondering if that was such a good idea, I guess."

"If it'll make you feel better, I'll go gargle," said Pamela.

"Go to sleep," I told her. "I may get up and go jogging tomorrow."

"I'll go with you," said Liz.

I was all mixed up as I fell asleep that night. Thinking of Pamela. Of Gwen. Of Mrs. Jones. Of Sam. Of everything we'd been talking about in the "Our Whole Lives" classes about respect and dignity and worth and meaning. . . .

20

What Happened at School

I woke early the next morning, and Liz got up with me, leaving Pamela on her side of our bed, head buried deep in her pillow. I hadn't said anything to Sam about going jogging, so he wasn't there. Brian and Tony and Hugh weren't early risers either.

We loved running in Central Park on that April morning. The air felt cold to me, and I wished I'd brought sweatpants instead of shorts because my legs were covered in goose bumps. But by the time we got to the park, spurred on by Mr. Corona's *"Hut . . . two, three, four . . . Hut . . . two, three, four . . . ,"* the sun was out and we were warm.

Liz and I didn't say anything more about Pamela. It's hard to talk when you're running, anyway, and I think we both just wanted to clear our heads and our lungs. We tried to fix parts of the skyline surrounding Central Park in our minds to keep our bearings—the Trump Hotel on the west,

Essex House on the South. . . . Only the dog walkers and joggers seemed to be out on Sunday morning. Traffic was light.

"I could . . . go for New York . . . if it was always . . . like this," I panted.

"Not me," Elizabeth puffed back. "I want to live in a. . . . Victorian house . . . in a little . . . New England town."

I just wanted to see more of the world. Feel more sophisticated. Be a little more daring. But I didn't want to be Pamela.

I liked the thought of a huge park in the heart of a city—Rock Creek Park in Washington, Central Park here in New York. We jogged past a lake, a boathouse, a carousel, a ballpark, tennis courts, even a zoo. Everything seemed to be sleeping. Even the ducks down on the water still had their heads tucked into their feathers.

Weird how a city could have such different personalities, I thought. One for night, one for early morning; one for weekdays, one for Sunday. Sort of like Pamela, maybe. Underneath she often seemed to me like she was sad and scared. And last night she was a party animal. No, not even that. A body part. A head.

Molly and Gwen were still sleeping when we got back, but we could hear Pamela gargling in the bathroom. When she came out, steam came with her. She was freshly showered and her hair was still damp.

"I wish I could just hang out with you guys today," I said as I slipped off my shorts and T-shirt and headed for the bathroom. "If I walk out that door and find Sam waiting . . ."

"I'll go get our breakfasts this time and bring them up," said Pamela.

I zipped in and out of the shower while she was gone, then turned it over to Liz, while Gwen and Molly, who just woke up, waited their turn.

When Pamela came back, she said, "Sam was downstairs and asked about you. I said you were sick."

"Sick?" I said.

"Well, you're sort of temporarily sick of him, aren't you?" she said.

"What did he say?" I asked.

"He wanted to know what was wrong with you, so I told him you were having bad cramps."

"Pamela, I was having bad cramps two weeks ago, and he knew it!" I said.

"So your periods are highly irregular," said Gwen, and we burst into laughter.

When we went out to the buses, Sam was waiting, as usual.

"You okay?" he asked.

"Yes," I told him. "Pamela's off her rocker."

"So I've been hearing," Sam said.

"What do you mean?"

"The usual. Gossip," he said, and let it ride. That was a conversation I didn't want to have.

I loved the Metropolitan Museum of Art. Sam and I were interested in different things, though. He wanted to hurry me along at displays where I wanted to linger. He finally wandered off with another group to see the Arms and Armor exhibit, and I could have spent half the day with the mummies in the Egyptian Art section. But then I would have missed the "seven centuries and five continents of fashionable dress" in the Costume Institute. The "ritual objects and articles of personal adornment" in Arts of Africa, Oceania, and the Americas. The manuscripts and carpets in Islamic Art.

Leave it to Brian, of course, to discover the lotus-handed fertility goddess from seventh-century India. When we came around a corner, he and a bunch of guys had gathered around one end of the glass case enclosing her, grinning and trying to get us girls to come over. Pamela had gone with that group, and she was hanging on to Hugh's arm, trying to be one of the guys. I wondered if her mom noticed how weird she was acting.

In the cafeteria later I didn't see Sam right away,

so I sat down with Gwen and Liz and Molly.

"Good! You can eat with us," said Liz, and we were even happier when Pamela joined us.

"Uh-oh. Spoke too soon," said Molly when we saw Sam enter from the other end of the cafeteria.

Suddenly Liz grabbed her sunglasses and stuck them over my ears. Then Molly picked up her baseball cap and pulled it down over my eyes, and—not to be outdone—Gwen, laughing, wrapped her sweater around my neck and chin. I sat perfectly still, trying not to laugh as Sam passed right by our table looking for me. Finally, though, he came back and figured it out. But he didn't think it was funny.

"I'm disappointed in you, Alice," he said, and walked away.

Disappointed?

"He's *disappointed* in me?" I croaked. "What am I? Five years old?" We burst out laughing. We couldn't help it.

Faith was eating with us, and it was worth listening to Sam spout off just to see her laugh. She'd been having a good time with Chris, from stage crew, all morning, and her smile seemed even brighter than before. But suddenly she turned to Pamela, and this time she looked serious.

"Pam, you probably should know—the guys

have been talking about you," she said.

"Me?" said Pamela. "I thought the focus was on Alice here." Then she added flippantly, "So who *don't* they talk about?"

"You know what they're saying, then?" Faith asked. "About you and Hugh?"

"So it was my first time!" Pamela said. "I'm not twelve anymore, you know."

Molly shrugged. "So *I'm* sixteen, and I've never even been kissed!" she said simply.

We all looked at Molly.

"Never?" said Liz.

"Unless you count a cousin who kissed me in a closet when we were seven," said Molly. "I've never had a boyfriend, either."

"But if you had a choice?" I questioned.

"Sure! I'd take one, if it was somebody great and I had the time and stage crew was over for the year and I didn't have Spanish Club and piano. It'll happen when it'll happen."

She meant it too, and I think we all envied her self-assurance. We had no doubt that Molly would have a boyfriend in college, if not before. It must be wonderful to be so content that you didn't need a "boyfriend badge" to wear everywhere you went, I thought.

I was beginning to feel a little ashamed of myself, though, for the way I'd been treating Sam. It was as if I wanted him to be around when I wanted company but wanted him gone when I didn't. We were scheduled for a special showing of a film on photography that afternoon in the museum's theater, and when I saw Sam stop at a watercooler before we went in, I walked over.

"Sam, I'm sorry," I said. "We were just cutting up."

But that wasn't what he'd been referring to. Sam straightened up and wiped his mouth. "You went out with a bunch of guys Friday night and didn't even tell me?" he said. "Okay, not just guys." Then he told me that rumors about a lot of kids had been floating around. We evidently weren't the only ones who went out. I guess that explained the notices under everyone's door that morning and why Mr. Corona had been sitting on a chair out in the hall all night.

"I didn't mention it to you because I thought you'd get upset, Sam," I said.

"So why didn't you try me?"

"All right, I'm sorry. I should have told you. Yesterday morning I should have said, 'A bunch of us went out last night and had a fantastic time.' Would you have felt better?"

"No."

"Hugh called our room and said there was a delivery for us at the front desk, and it would take three or four girls to carry it—that we should come down and pick it up."

"And you *believed* that?"

"I didn't know who it was! I didn't even know Hugh! He has a deep voice! When we got off the elevator, he and Brian and Tony were waiting, and—"

"Tony was there too?"

"Yes. Hugh's brother used to go to NYU and he knew some places around there we could go, so we went. If you'd been there, we would have included you. It's just something that happened!"

"And that's supposed to make it okay?"

"What did I do that was so wrong?" I asked.

He looked at me like I'd asked if two plus two equals four. "Your attitude, for starters. How would you have felt if *I'd* gone out with a bunch of girls and guys and didn't tell you?"

"I would have said, 'Bravo! Did you have a good time?'"

We stood facing each other for a moment or two. What Sam was saying made sense, and what I was feeling made sense too. It was what we'd been talking about at church—about me being responsible, on the one hand, and a need in me to be more spontaneous, on the other. I didn't want to go so far in one direction that I was practically getting engaged-to-be-engaged to Sam Mayer, but

I didn't want to lean so far in the other that I was giving head to a guy just because he had a big chest and curly hair and might possibly invite me to the prom.

"Maybe we just might have to agree to disagree here, Sam," I told him. "I think I'm a little more spontaneous than you are, and I don't like to have to keep explaining myself to you."

"Maybe you are," he said, "but I forgive you," and kissed me, and we were right back to square one. But he did leave me alone after that and let me sit with the girls in the theater after I promised to sit with him on the bus back home.

The United Nations that afternoon, our final event of the trip, made me forget Sam. Made me forget Pamela and school and the rest of my world back in Silver Spring temporarily. I hadn't expected to be floored. First the sight of that tall narrow building I'd seen so often in photos. Then those 191 flags of each member state. But it was the sculpture we saw at the entrance, a gun with its barrel twisted into a knot, that made me want to take its picture and send it to everyone I knew. What an elegant way to make such an important statement. No guns. No war. No killing. If only it were that simple. . . .

I don't know which impressed me more, the photos on Ellis Island or our tour of the UN. Here at UN Headquarters was the General Assembly room, the Security Council meeting room—I'd seen them on TV when groups were in session. Here I was. And here, in display cases in one of the corridors, were coins, tin cans, and bottles that had melted in the atomic blasts in Japan and, on the wall, a photo of a small child, dead and hideously burned in the inferno.

But as we went back outside to board the buses for home, there were Brian Brewster and Tony Osler, cutting up. There was Charlene Verona with her eyelash curler, checking her makeup. There I was, sliding into a seat beside Sam, going back to my same old neighborhood, same old school. Same old self?

I was pretty quiet for a while after I boarded, and Sam just sat with his arm around me and let me be. He probably thought I was tired, which I was, but I didn't want to go back home the same as I'd started. I wanted to feel I had changed somehow—that the trip had changed me. I mean, everything around me was changing. Dad got married and was getting on with his life; Lester had moved out and was getting on with his. Pamela, across the aisle, was sitting on Hugh's lap again—whether invited or uninvited, I wasn't quite sure—and for better or worse, she was getting on with hers. Was I going to be Alice

Forever—the same yesterday, today, and tomorrow?

The infamous plastic boxes were waiting for us on board—our dinner—with their cold macaroni salad and little tins of tuna and lemon squares and two cherry tomatoes each. We ate halfheartedly, yet I couldn't help but think that each box would be a feast to a starving family in much of the world.

We figured the teachers would want to get us back to Silver Spring as soon as possible so we wouldn't be too tired at school the next day. We were surprised, then, when the buses just sat there idling their motors. Five forty-five. Five fifty. . . .

"What are we waiting for?" someone called out.

Suddenly Mr. Corona came on board. "Pamela Jones?" he called.

Pamela slid off Hugh's lap and stood up. "Yeah?" she said.

"Do you happen to know where your mother is?" he asked.

I heard Pamela exhale. "No," she said. "Is she missing?"

"Well, it appears she is. You two roomed together. Was everything all right this morning?"

"I . . . I think so," Pamela said.

"Well . . ." Mr. Corona looked at the rest of us. He was in no mood for this, I could tell, having been up all night. "Anybody see Mrs. Jones in the UN building?"

"I saw her at lunch back at the museum," Karen called out.

"I did too," said someone else.

Mr. Corona looked at Pamela again, then at his watch. "We've got security guards checking the restrooms," he said. "We don't want to get started much later than this."

Pamela stepped back and slowly sank down in a seat beside Liz. "I . . . will . . . die . . . of . . . humiliation," she murmured.

Mr. Corona got back off the bus and stood out on the sidewalk talking with another teacher. Just then a taxi pulled up in front of us, and Mrs. Jones got out. She was holding a small white bag and came hurrying over to Mr. Corona. We couldn't hear what she was saying, but she was gesturing with her hands. Then at the little sack. She looked embarrassed. Mr. Corona motioned her toward the other bus with the second teacher, then he got on ours. The doors closed and the buses pulled out.

He came back to where Pamela was sitting. "She was trying to get a prescription refilled and had a hard time finding a drugstore, so she had to take a cab," he said. "Everything's okay. Relax." And he went back up to sit behind the driver.

I looked back at Pamela.

"I didn't know she was taking medicine,"

Pamela said. "Why didn't she bring enough in the first place?"

"Maybe she needed more than she thought," I said.

Sam was tugging at me to settle down and concentrate on him, so I did. Hugh and Tony were sitting together, and Pamela was trying to squeeze in between them now. Hugh was somewhat playfully—I think—pushing Pamela away. It was sort of pathetic. She finally gave up and went back to sit with Liz again, and as she left he gave her a slap on the butt, and that seemed to please her.

Sam put his arm around me, and in spite of everything, it had a welcoming feel. It was nice to slip temporarily out of the real world and into Sam's. Nice to feel a protective arm around you when you've overdosed on tenements and atomic bombs and "Desperate Girls."

The lights dimmed so that the driver could see the road better. A few kids up front were laughing and kidding around with Mr. Corona as they ate, but most of us were pretty zonked, and a few were actually asleep. We could hear somebody's CD player—a mellow song—and I put my head on Sam's shoulder.

"I love you," he whispered in my ear.

My eyes popped open. I didn't move. I couldn't

say it back because I didn't think I did. I really *liked* him, but love?

He didn't try to get me to say it. He just kissed me—slowly and tenderly—and his hand touched the skin under my shirt.

What did I like most? I asked myself. Sam or what he was doing? I kissed him back, and he was grateful. He covered us both with his jacket, and our hands explored each other beneath the denim.

It was almost eleven o'clock when the buses pulled in the school parking lot. I think we were all late to school the next day.

When I saw Pamela at her locker the next morning, she said, "Mom slipped me this note last night."

I sat down on a nearby bench and read the piece of paper:

> Pamela,
> I'm sorry about all this. I
> shouldn't have gone on this
> trip without asking you, and
> I know I embarrassed you
> by being There. I've been
> having some anxiety attacks
> lately, and the doctor had
> given me pills, but I guess

I needed more than I had with me, and a lot of the drugstores were closed. Please forgive me.
Mom

I looked at Pamela. "So why don't you?" I asked.

"What? Forgive her?" She took the note back and stuffed it in a pocket. "Maybe," she said.

Two things happened at school later that day.

At lunch in the cafeteria Hugh was sitting two tables over with some other seniors. When Pamela saw him, she set her tray down on our table and immediately started toward him. When I saw the look on Hugh's face as Pamela approached, she made me think of a baby teetering too close to the top of the stairs. You don't know what's going to happen, but you know what *might* and you aren't close enough to stop it.

With no encouragement from Hugh, Pamela brazenly plunked herself down on his lap and put her arms playfully around his neck—the way she'd done on the subway. The bus. Before when she'd done it, he had slapped her thigh, patted her bottom, run his hands up and down her sides.

This time, however, there wasn't even a glimmer of an invitation on his face. He leaned stiffly back as she settled between him and his lunch tray. "Do I know you?" I heard him say.

"Do you *know* me?" Pamela said in answer, leaning forward to brush his lips. I'm not sure what she said to him next, but I *think* it was "I'd say you know me very well."

The other guys at the table were looking at her in pained silence.

Pamela gave Hugh's neck a little jerk with her hands. "Hey! Studly! Liven up!" she said.

Hugh just stared back at her. "C'mon," he said, his voice low. "Get off." He didn't touch her. His arms remained at his sides.

Get off, Pamela! I wanted to scream. *Just come back to our table!* She didn't.

"What's the matter?" she asked.

"Please get off," Hugh said.

Instead, Pamela began that same wiggle she'd done on the subway when she pretended she was lap dancing, watching Hugh's eyes all the while.

"I can't watch," Gwen whispered, shielding her eyes.

Suddenly Hugh pushed back and stood up, and Pamela tumbled off, almost falling to the floor. She stared at him incredulously, but Hugh just sat back down, leaned his elbows on the table so she couldn't get in his lap again, and continued his conversation with his buddies, while they gave Pamela an embarrassed smile.

Pamela righted herself, her face flaming. I'd never seen it so red. I could barely look at her, and Liz and Gwen quickly began talking as though they hadn't seen anything. Pamela came back to our table and ate half her lunch, head down, then threw the rest away. She left the cafeteria and I followed. She was heading straight for the restroom, and when I got inside, she was crying, big helpless sobs.

There was nothing to say that she didn't already know. I just went over and put my arms around her. She leaned against me crying like a little kid. Crying . . . and crying . . . and crying. It was more than just Hugh. It was the whole way her life had been going lately.

"S-so humiliating!" she wept finally.

"I know," I said. "I know."

But the worst was yet to come, and it didn't involve Pamela. Have you ever had a sad day just get sadder? I was worried all afternoon about Pamela. All I wanted to think about, concentrate on, was Pamela and how I might help. But Sam followed me around like a puppy. He wanted to know if I was mad that *he* was mad that I had gone out with friends in New York. I thought we had been through all that, and I was glad that he didn't have his mom's car, or else we'd have had to continue that conversation after school.

Instead, it was Molly who had her dad's car that day and offered to give Liz and me a ride home. She had to stop at the office first, though, and pay the balance on her trip to New York. When we went out the back door to the parking lot finally, most of the kids had left. We had just started across the lot when we saw Faith backed up against Ron's Toyota, crying, and Ron had both hands on her shoulders.

"Admit it!" he was yelling.

"Ron, I swear!" Faith said.

"Damn it, I'm not stupid! Say you were with him!"

"No!" Faith, still crying, jerked herself free and turned away.

And suddenly, while we stared in disbelief, Ron grabbed her by the back of the neck and slammed her face down, hard, on the hood of his car.

"Oh my God!" I cried. We started to run.

"Stop it!" Molly yelled. "Get away from her!"

For a moment it looked as though Faith was going down on her knees, but then she grabbed on to the car, and when she lifted her head, her face was a bloody mess.

Ron stepped back, staring at her, and then we were all over him, pulling him away. Faith's eyes were scrunched up in pain, one hand over her mouth and a hurt, howling sound coming from her throat.

"Faith!" Ron cried. "I didn't mean to! I'm sorry!"

Faith held out one arm to hold him at bay, the other covered with blood from her mouth and nose. I was holding her up on one side, Elizabeth on the other, and Molly had her cell phone out, dialing 911. We took Faith to the office and didn't leave her side.

In the principal's office, the nurse fished two teeth out of Faith's mouth, caught between her lip and her gum. The principal had found Ron sitting in his car in the parking lot, and the two officers who answered the call brought him into the office.

"Miss," the first officer said to Faith, "this the fellow who did that to you?"

Faith was holding a wet towel against her mouth. She nodded, her eyes barely open, her face swollen and beginning to bruise.

"And we're witnesses!" I added.

"Faith, you need to press charges," said the principal.

"Oh, jeez!" I heard Molly whisper. "Don't ask her to do that! Just *take* him!"

But one of the policemen said, "She doesn't

need to file charges. When there's obvious evidence of an assault, that's all we need to take him in."

"Take him in," said Faith, turning her face away.

I wanted to cheer.

"Faith, I *love* you!" Ron protested, starting toward her, but the officer held him back.

"Buddy, you sure have a strange way of showing it," the man said. "Come on. Let's get in the car."

The principal phoned Faith's father to tell him that he was taking her to the emergency room. He carried the two teeth in a little bottle of salt water, in case they could be reattached somehow. After Faith left, Molly, Liz, and I sat in Molly's car, stunned by what we had seen.

"The problem is, will she relent later and take him back?" I wondered aloud.

"Maybe she can get a restraining order so he can't come near her," said Liz.

"If Ron comes near her again, they'll have to restrain *me*!" Molly said, her eyes fierce with anger.

When I got home later, Dad was still at work. Sylvia had a parent conference, but Lester was there, rummaging through the fridge.

"Well, look at you!" I said, plunking my books on the table. "He comes over when no one's home and steals the food."

"Wrong!" said Lester. "I figure I've mooched off you guys enough, so *I'm* cooking dinner tonight. Chicken diablo. How does that sound?"

"Anything sounds good after today," I said, and told him what had happened out in the parking lot. I *almost* told him what happened to Pamela, but then I'd have to explain what she'd done to Hugh in New York, and I wanted to be loyal to Pamela. I did tell him about her mother coming on our trip uninvited, though, and what I'd seen at the UN.

"Does the world get better, Les, or does it just go around and around with the same problems happening all over again?" I asked. "I can't believe what Ron did to Faith. I just want to move to a place where things like this can't happen."

"Where women don't have teeth?"

"Where guys can't knock them out, Lester! Be serious for once! I want to live in a place where people don't kill each other and mothers can be forgiven and guys aren't so needy and girls don't do everything a guy wants and—"

"Whooooa!" Les said, turning around and studying me hard. "What's this?"

I did a quick retreat. "Just . . . Sam. He's just always around wanting more and more and more—"

"Of *what*? You trying to tell me something?"

"Me! My time! I mean, he's always *around*! He's always waiting for me. He says he *loves* me, Lester! We've only been going out for two months!"

"Hmmm." Lester put the chicken on a bed of rice and slid the pan in the oven. "Well, a guy can't help how he feels. And you can't help how you feel about *him*. Just make sure you're honest with him. Don't say something just to make him happy."

"Or *do* something . . . ," I said.

Lester gave me a quizzical frown. "Or *do* something!" he repeated emphatically.

The dentist couldn't reattach Faith's teeth, and she was out of school for a week while her face healed and she was fitted for a bridge. When she came back with a temporary bridge in her mouth, it was difficult for her to smile even if she'd wanted. We knew she was still in pain. But all of us on stage crew rallied around her, and the guys were like German shepherds, they were so protective of her—Chris, in particular. I think maybe she was ready to move on, but you can never tell about girls like Faith. Ron had been arrested on assault charges, but that was still up in the air.

I was thinking about what we'd discussed in that "Our Whole Lives" class—about questions to ask yourself before you have intercourse.

Questions like, *Do I trust my partner completely?* Maybe you should ask yourself some of those questions before you even take on a *boyfriend,* I thought. Maybe you should ask yourself if you are truly comfortable in that person's presence, or if you always feel you're on the defensive. If one of you is always the giver and the other the taker. If you often feel you'd rather just be alone. And maybe, though he's worlds away from Ron, I should be asking those same questions about Sam and me.

21

Party?

As soon as I'd come back from New York, I'd signed up for the driver training course so I could at least start it before my birthday on May 14. Dad let me have time off work on Saturday mornings.

I carried the *Maryland Driver's Handbook* with me wherever I went, and it seemed like I was studying for my SAT. I'd hand the book to anyone—Liz in the cafeteria, Sam in his car, Gwen in the library, Pamela on my porch—and say, "Ask me anything."

"True or false," Gwen might say. "When approaching a cyclist on the road ahead of you, you should sound your horn to let him know you are there."

"False," I said. "You'd startle him."

"How many feet in advance do you start signaling before making a turn?" Sam might ask.

"One hundred." I had it down pat.

My driving instructor, Mr. Higgins, was a man entirely lacking in humor. He would take three of us out at a time—two in the backseat, one at the wheel—and then we'd trade off. One of the students was a guy who must have been six feet seven. His head cleared the roof of the car by a half inch. The other, a girl who always wore a brown sweater, reminded me of a little mouse because she squeaked and squealed when she got nervous.

If she was trying to make a turn downtown and pedestrians were crossing in front of her, she'd inch the car forward but squeal and slam on the brakes each time someone else crossed. Inch her way forward and squeal again. Kenny—the tall guy—and I would sit in back desperately trying not to laugh, and once he even stuffed a tennis ball in his mouth to block the sound. That made me laugh out loud.

Mr. Higgins never laughed at anything. We saw his eyes watching us from the dual rearview mirrors. "You two won't think it's funny when you go for your driving test and don't know your ass from your elbow," he said. "You pay attention, you might learn something." And then he'd be extra hard on me or Kenny when one of us was in the driver's seat next, and I guess we deserved it.

"Four little words, and you can't read 'em," he said to me. "'No turn on red.' Which of those words don't you understand?"

. . .

A week before my birthday Dad asked, "What should we plan for your sixteenth, Al? This is a biggie, right?"

This, of course, meant he hadn't planned anything yet at all. His own birthday had come and gone, and I'd only bought him a book and some candy. I felt guilty even suggesting something. What I wanted most, of course, next to world peace, was my driver's license, yet I couldn't even begin to parallel park.

"I don't know, Dad," I said about my birthday. "Surprise me."

"Do you want a party?" he asked.

"Sure. I want to wear a beaded gown and a feather headdress and enter on the back of an elephant," I answered.

"Seriously? A party?" he said.

"Not if I have to plan it," I told him. I just wished I could click my heels together, whirl around three times, and be sixteen, without the fuss and bother. Or did I? To make matters worse, my birthday was on a Saturday this year, and half the kids I knew were working weekends.

Lester took me out a couple more times for driving lessons, but he was busy too, and each hour he spent with me was one hour less he might have spent with Tracy. For some reason, learning to drive was harder for me than I'd expected, and I could tell that Les felt I should be catching on sooner than I did.

Between school and church and driver's training and the orthodontist and Sam, I hardly had any time for myself. What little I had left over I tried to reserve for Pamela. She had looked forward to New York so much, and now she seemed to have shrunk back into the shadows. With Brian and Tony and some of the other guys, who gave her knowing looks and made suggestive comments, she was brash and flirty, but around us we could see that sad and desperate look we knew so well.

She'd sit through a class with her mind a million miles away. Go home from school and take a nap. A lot of times I'd call and could tell I'd woken her up. We'd all been worried about Faith, and now even Faith was concerned about Pamela.

I decided I had enough to worry about without trying to get my license the day after I turned sixteen. I would simply put it out of my mind, get more practice with Dad or Les, and go in for my test when I felt up to it. Forget the calendar. Besides, I didn't want to ruin my birthday celebration, whatever it was going to be. Neither Dad nor Sylvia had said one word about a party on Saturday, and if they'd been planning one, I should have known by now. As for my friends, when a birthday falls on the weekend, we usually celebrate it on Friday at school.

Friends are supposed to go all out on your birthday. They usually decorate your locker with balloons and streamers and ribbons. They'll even wallpaper the inside sometimes. They'll bring you flowers and Hershey's bars and teddy bears.

It's fun if you have a lot of friends. It's not so fun if you don't. The *really* popular kids get tons of stuff and walk around all day loaded down with it to show how popular they are. I hung out with the really popular crowd only once, in seventh grade, when a bunch of us called ourselves the "Famous Eight." But we weren't famous for long, and I've never tried to be Miss Popularity since. But I was really disappointed when I rounded the corner to my locker on Friday. There was Sam, holding a bunch of cellophane-wrapped flowers, but my locker door was as bare as a baby's bottom.

Nothing. No notes, no balloons, no ribbons or streamers. I was afraid I might cry, silly as it was, or that Sam would see the disappointment on my face.

"Oh, thanks! You remembered!" I said.

"How could I forget?" he said, and kissed me.

I turned the combination on my lock. *Maybe they decorated the inside,* I thought. *I'll bet when I open the door, a sea of balloons will float out.* I opened the door. Nothing. Just a few books and a forgotten sweater.

"Do you want your present now or later?" Sam asked, smiling.

"Now is fine," I said, really wanting to go straight home and crawl into bed. This meant that there was no party planned for tomorrow or Sam would have waited till then. He wanted me to have at least *some*thing to show my friends, even if he was the only one who remembered.

He handed me two little boxes wrapped together with a single gold ribbon and bow. I opened the smaller one on top—a miniature box from Godiva of six chocolates in the shape of clamshells and mushrooms that smelled more like perfume than chocolate.

The larger box was heavier, and when I lifted the lid, I found a small framed photo of Sam and me, taken by his mom at their condo the night of the dance. It was a good photo. We both look either deliriously happy or slightly manic, depending on your interpretation. What was the matter with me? I wondered. Why didn't I feel a rush of love for this wonderful, caring guy?

"Oh, Sam," I said. I was embarrassed to feel a tear roll down my cheek.

He reached over and kissed it. "I'm sentimental too," he said. "Mom gave me an enlargement, and

I've got it on my wall above the bed." I felt even worse.

As I headed for class, though, I had another thought. *If nobody wishes me happy birthday—if no one says anything at all about it—I'll know they're up to something,* I decided. But they *did* mention it.

"Happy birthday, Alice," said Liz. "Are your dad and Sylvia going to take you somewhere special tomorrow?"

"Happy b-day!" called Pamela when we passed in the hall.

"Heeey! Sweet sixteen and she's sweeeeeet!" yelled Mark Stedmeister.

It's when *friends,* who *know* how much a birthday is supposed to mean to you, especially this one, let you down that you really feel awful. Hadn't I baked brownies for Pamela on birthdays in the past? Hadn't I traded earrings with Liz? Didn't they remember all the times I'd tied balloons to the handles of their lockers? The cards? The candy? Was this old hat, now that we were growing up? Just freshman stuff?

I wanted the day to end. All afternoon I watched the clock, and when the last bell rang, I went to my locker, fully expecting to see Sam waiting for me, ready to give me a ride home. But he wasn't. Even Sam, it seemed, had run out of steam. I opened the locker, and there was a little piece of folded paper on the floor, on top of a pair of old running shoes. *Probably Sam apologizing for not having the car today,* I thought.

I unfolded the paper and recognized Pamela's handwriting:

> Important! There's a note for you at the front office.

I stared at it. Now what? Something about her mom, I guessed. I was going to get caught up in some new mother/daughter conflict. Have to testify for what I saw or didn't see her do in New York.

The office was on the other side of the school, and as I made the long trek down the hall and then down the stairs to the first floor, I wondered if it had to do with Faith instead. Maybe Liz and I, as witnesses, were going to have to testify in court against Ron, but then, why wouldn't this note have been from Liz?

I went into the office. "Did someone leave a note for me?" I asked. "Alice McKinley?"

"Yep. Right here," said the clerk, and handed me a small white envelope with my name on it. Liz's careful printing, with the daisy she always uses to dot the *i* in *Alice*. *What* is *this?* I wondered, and opened the envelope.

• • •

Important! Go to the Pizza Hut across the street. Ask for Mike and say, "McKinley."

By now I'd missed my bus, but I didn't care. The gloom that had settled over me all day suddenly lifted, and I laughed out loud as I walked outside.

The Pizza Hut was actually a half block away, but I trotted obediently down the sidewalk. I thought I saw Molly down at the far corner holding her cell phone to her ear, but she slipped behind a parked car and I wasn't sure.

Inside the Pizza Hut, I half expected the gang to yell, *Surprise!* It was full of students, but none of the friends in our crowd. I waited my turn in line, then said, "Is Mike here?"

The older of the two guys came over. "Yeah?" he said.

"McKinley," I said.

"Oh, yeah!" He grinned and reached into the pocket of his shirt and pulled out a paper, neatly folded into smaller and smaller squares. "Here you are," he said.

I took it back outside.

Important! Go to the library on Colesville Road and look up

"sex" in the World Book
Encyclopedia

"You guys!" I hooted when I saw Liz and Pamela behind the shrubbery up ahead, but they just ducked and laughed, so I went on over to Colesville Road and down the hill to the library. Brian and Mark were pretending to read newspapers in the magazine section. I figured I'd been watched since I opened the first note.

I went into the reference room, but they told me that the *World Book Encyclopedia* was in the children's section. When I went there, a large boy with one finger up his right nostril had the *S* volume opened on the table and was laboriously copying a whole passage from an article on satellites.

"Is this the only *World Book* set that you have?" I asked the librarian.

"I'm afraid so," she said. "But we have the newest edition of *Encyclopædia Britannica*. What did you want to look up?"

"Uh . . . never mind," I said, and went back to sit across from the boy whose finger must have got stuck up his nose, because it was still there.

How long had he had the volume? I wondered. What if he'd found the note and read it? What if he'd thrown it away?

"Excuse me," I said to him finally. "Could I look up something in that book? I'll give it right back to you."

The boy slowly raised his head, dislodged his finger, and licked it. I tried not to gag. "You can have it when I'm done," he said, and went on writing.

I saw Molly and Gwen watching from the doorway, hands over their mouths.

"It's sort of urgent," I said to the boy.

"So is this," he said. "My aunt's going to pick me up in ten minutes, and I've got to have this done."

I reached in my backpack for my change purse and held up a quarter. "Could I have it for just a minute?"

He stared at the quarter, shook his head, and went on writing. This time I *knew* I heard Molly laugh.

I dug around in my backpack for my wallet and pulled out a dollar. "Can I have it for just a *second*?" I asked, waving it in front of his eyes. If he didn't take it, I was going to snatch the encyclopedia out from under his nose.

He looked at me like I was a crazy person. "Okay," he said, and took the dollar.

I quickly looked up *sex* and at first didn't see the note, because it was folded into tiny pleats so that it was thin as a pencil, tucked deep into the crease of the binding.

"Thanks," I said, and slid the book back to him.

Now he was really staring. "Are you a spy?" he asked, wide-eyed.

"Something like that," I told him, and heard my friends laugh as I scooted my chair out from the table and left the library with an entourage behind me: Pamela, Gwen, Elizabeth, Molly, Sam, Mark, and Brian. I opened the piece of paper:

> Go to Starbucks and look for a note taped to the underside of the table by the window.

How long had it taken them to work this out? I wondered. Had they all stayed after school just for this? We were all laughing as I entered Starbucks.

The shop was full. Every table was taken—people drinking coffee and reading newspapers and munching scones. I looked toward the table by the window. A thirty-something couple sat there deep in conversation, their eyes only on each other, hands interlocked. From where I stood, I noticed that the woman had slipped off one shoe and was running her toes slowly up under the man's right trouser leg.

"You *guys!*" I whispered, giggling. "How am I going to interrupt?"

"Go for it!" said Pamela. "It's your birthday!"

I made my way over to the window. "Excuse me," I said.

They looked up at me impatiently without answering.

"I think there's something under the table meant for me," I said. "Would you mind if I took a look, just for a second?"

"What?" said the man.

"I just have to crawl under your table for a minute," I said.

I could tell that the woman was desperately fishing around for her shoe.

"Couldn't you come back later?" the man said. "We're having a conversation here."

"Please don't stop," I said. "I'll just take a quick look and leave." I couldn't *believe* I had the nerve, and I probably never would have done it if I hadn't had an audience egging me on.

The couple stared in disbelief as I crawled between their legs under the table. A piece of paper was taped to the underside. I pulled and it tore in half.

Now the manager was coming over.

"Could you do something about the girl under our table?" the woman said indignantly.

I was desperately trying to pull off the other half of the note. I saw an upside-down face peering at me, scowling.

"Miss?" the manager said sternly. Everyone in Starbucks was staring now.

I got the other half of the paper and crawled out, and the gang by the door whooped and cheered. We went outside where I unfolded the last piece of paper:

Go directly home. Do not pass Go.
Do not collect $200. Let's party!

"*Yes!*" I said. "You guys are the best!"

Sam and Brian and Molly all had cars, so we piled in, and a few minutes later we pulled up in front of my house, where Karen and Jill were waiting. I saw that both Dad's and Sylvia's cars were there and knew that they must have been in on the secret too.

I couldn't believe who all showed up, and they seemed to keep coming. Penny and Lori and Leslie and, my God, even Patrick!

The gifts were small and silly: a little bottle of champagne delivered in an old sneaker; a scented candle; crazy socks; thong panties (two pair) from Liz and Pamela; a snow globe with her picture inside from Gwen; a miniature bubble gum machine. There were cards, too, from friends who couldn't make it. Even Rosalind.

Dad and Sylvia had put out a buffet of Mexican food from my favorite Tex-Mex restaurant, and we took our plastic plates and forks and spread out in the living room, most of us on the floor. It was like a big picnic.

Molly told Dad and Sylvia about the treasure hunt and how I had to bribe the boy in the library. "He was, like, 'No! Get your own!'" she said, and Dad chuckled.

But when Gwen told them how I had to crawl under the table at Starbucks—"And the woman was trying to get her shoe back on . . ."—both Dad and Sylvia threw back their heads in laughter.

"What scared us most was the encyclopedia," said Pamela. "When we saw the kid go pick it up right after I'd put the note in it, we were afraid he'd find it."

"When *did* you take those notes around?" I asked.

"We were on our cell phones, one step ahead of you the whole way," said Liz.

The party had started right after school and didn't end till about seven. People began to drift off after that, and others stayed to help clean up. I hugged every single person, even Patrick. "This is the best party yet," I said. "I hope you guys know how much I love you."

"And you thought we'd forgotten you," said Liz. "We've been planning this party the whole week!"

I got kissed by almost everyone there too. Sam was no surprise, but when Patrick left, he kissed my cheek, and I'll admit there was still some zing. Sam probably noticed. But, hey, it was my birthday, and you're only sixteen once.

Faith called that evening to wish me a happy birthday too. She'd had another dental appointment after school so had to miss the celebration. I could tell she was still in pain, but we were getting used to her speaking slower.

"How are things going?" I asked. "Liz and I will testify if you want us to."

"Oh, thanks," she said, "but I don't think I'll need that. Ron has to pay a fine, all my dental expenses, and attend an anger management course. He started yesterday, I think."

I had that sinking, hopeless feeling. "But . . . if he starts hanging around again?" I asked.

"Uh-uh. I think he finally understands. But my parents want me to see a counselor during the summer to find out . . . well, why I was attracted to a guy who would knock my teeth out."

I went from hopeless to hopeful. "I'm glad," I

said. "Because . . . well, Ron might want to talk you into going out together again."

"Not on the agenda," Faith told me. "Besides, I'm sort of going out with Chris now. We had a really good time in New York."

22

Decision

"Oh, Les, you missed the best party!" I said later, when he stopped by with my present.

"Yeah? I heard about the Mexican food," said Lester. "Any left?"

"I put a whole platter away for you," Sylvia said, and slid it in the microwave.

I sat down across from Lester while he ate. "What is it?" I asked, holding his gift in my lap.

"Now, why do people always say that? Open it and see!" said Lester.

I took off the paper and lifted the lid. There was the most gorgeous silk robe. It was a heavenly shade of turquoise with a mandarin collar and decorative button loops in front.

"Lester, it's beautiful!" I said. "You never gave me clothes before!"

"You were never sixteen before," he said. "You just never know what a sixteen-year-old girl is going to do, and I figure if I give you something to wear, at least you won't run around naked." Then he added, "Actually, Tracy helped me pick it out."

I stood up and slipped it on over my jeans and T-shirt, loving the way the silk draped over my body. I had no idea when or where I would wear this, but just knowing that something so beautiful, so adult, would be hanging in my closet gave me a thrill.

"Now, doesn't *she* look sophisticated!" said Sylvia.

"*Thank* you!" I told Lester. I went around the table and kissed him. "You know what Dad gave me? A check for a hundred and sixty dollars!"

Lester gave a whistle. "What are you going to do with it?"

"Save it for a special trip or something. And Sylvia gave me a beaded purse to take to dances."

"Which reminds me," said Lester. "Are we supposed to dress up for Marilyn's wedding next month? There was a message on my answering machine from her. All she said was 'Bring a guest.'"

"Your dad's wearing a suit and tie," Sylvia said.

"Are you going to bring Tracy?" I asked Lester.

"Of course," he said.

I wondered who I should bring. I didn't want to tag along with Dad and Sylvia all evening. I didn't want to come as Lester's little sister, either. But the thought of inviting *Sam* to a *wedding* . . . like we were a *couple* . . .

The phone rang and Sylvia said suddenly, "I'll bet that's your aunt Sally, Alice. She got the dates mixed up and thought your birthday was today. She called earlier during your party, and said she'd call back."

I went down the hall and picked up the phone. It was Aunt Sally.

"Oh my goodness, there is my sixteen-year-old niece!" she said. "Why, Alice, you even *sound* more grown up."

"Thank you," I said.

"Carol chose your birthday gift, but we didn't get it mailed until yesterday. It's a big box of bath oils and soaps and powders, Alice. I'm just telling you this in case something leaks."

I smiled. "I'll enjoy it no matter what," I said.

"Well!" There was a pause. Aunt Sally always gets the superficial stuff out of the way first, and then her worries take over. "Sylvia told me you were having a party when I called before. So how does a sixteen-year-old girl celebrate nowadays?"

I told her about the treasure hunt and the Tex-Mex food and the silly little presents.

"Oh, Alice, that sounds like good pure fun!" she gushed gratefully.

The "pure" bothered me a little, so I decided to head her off at the pass and change the subject. "I'm getting ready to take my driver's test," I said. "Wish me luck."

"Oh, I forgot all about driving! Now, Alice, you know what can happen to a girl in a car, don't you?"

Did Aunt Sally ever think of anything besides sex? I wondered. "Yeah," I said. "She could run off the road."

"All sorts of things, dear. Don't ever drive in fog, Alice. And if you're in a bad rainstorm, just pull over to the side of the road and put your emergency blinker on. If the car breaks down and a man stops and asks if he can help, don't roll down your window. And here's a little safety hint. If a man ever comes to your window with a gun and tries to get in the car with you, pretend you're having a heart attack and fall over on the horn. Just plop right over as hard as you can and let that horn blow. That's what I told Carol when she was learning to drive, and she hasn't had to use it so far, but it just might save your life some day."

"I'll remember that, Aunt Sally," I said.

When I hung up and went back to the kitchen, a wide smile on my face, I said, "Les, do you remember when Aunt Sally used to tell us to wear red corks on a string around our necks when we went swimming? So that if we were ever floating unconscious beneath the water, the cork would bob about on top and someone might rescue us?"

Lester grinned. "No, but I remember her telling me that if I was out with a crowd and somebody handed me a beer, I should take it in the bathroom, pour it down the toilet, replace it with water, and no one would ever know."

We laughed. "Well, now she wants me to fake a heart attack and fall over on the horn if a man ever tries to get in my car."

"Well, for Pete's sake, make sure it's not me trying to get in, or *I'll* be the one having a heart attack," said Lester.

I spent my actual birthday taking my driving lesson and then doing my usual routine at the Melody Inn. Everyone made a fuss over me, of course. But the following Saturday I had to go to the orthodontist before I went to work in the afternoon.

"Go ahead," I said ruefully. "Tighten the wires and make me miserable."

"For an ordinarily pretty girl, you do a lot of complaining," he said.

I shut up then because I wasn't sure what he meant. Had he meant "extraordinarily pretty" or "pretty in an ordinary way" or "pretty ordinary"? It gave me something to think about while he worked on my teeth, and I took a Tylenol as soon as he was done to head off the soreness in my mouth. I even managed to say "Thanks" as I left the office.

"Now, *that's* a change!" he said.

Once again, without my asking him, Sam was there in the waiting room to drive me to the Melody Inn.

"I told Dad I'd take the bus," I said.

"Well, I figure any girl whose teeth are hurting needs a ride," he said.

"I thought you were working for your mom this weekend," I told him.

"I am, but she'll always give me time off to see you," he said.

I shut up then, and we rode in silence for a while. Then Sam looked over at me and said, "Sometimes I get the feeling you're not too happy to see me, Alice."

I didn't want this conversation today. "My mouth is sore, that's all."

"Sometimes even when it's not sore," he said, and this time he stared straight ahead.

"It's just that . . . that sometimes . . . sometimes I sort of feel you're smothering me, Sam." I couldn't believe I'd actually said that. Even after I said the words, they seemed to echo around in the car.

"Loving you . . . is smothering you?"

"Sam, I just don't know how I feel about *you*!"

"That's okay," he said. Then he added, "Mom really likes you. She says maybe you're about the best thing that ever happened to me."

I turned and looked at him. "Sam, she doesn't even know me! Not really!"

"Sure she does. I've told her all about you."

"You run everything by your mom?"

"Well . . ." He grinned a little. "Not *everything*."

"Look," I said desperately. "I can't honestly say that I love you."

"I can wait."

I leaned back against the seat and closed my eyes. "That's just what I'm talking about! You're almost *too* nice! You're . . . you're always *here*! Always kissing me, looking after me . . ."

"Well, excuse *me*! I thought that's what a girl wanted in a guy." His voice took on a different tone.

"Well, it is . . . and it isn't. Not twenty-four/seven."

"So what *do* you want?" he asked, and he was angry this time. Sam angry was better than Sam hurt, I decided. "The tough guy, like Ron? You want to be knocked around a little?"

"No."

"Then *what*?"

"I don't know, but it doesn't have to be either/or. You don't have to either follow me around like a puppy or knock me around." I stared out the side window. "There's more to life than us, Sam. I just . . . want *you* to get a life too. Apart from me, I mean."

"I was sort of hoping I might have a life *with* you," he said.

And that, I guess, is when it happened. Right there in Sam's car, two blocks from the Melody Inn on a busy Saturday morning, stuck in traffic. I said, "Sam, this just isn't working. I'm really very sorry."

Sam's face actually turned pale. Like the blood had drained out of it. It frightened me for a moment.

"Alice, you can't mean that. Remember the bus ride home from New York?"

I remembered it all too well. Touching each other under Sam's jacket. What guy *wouldn't* have thought it was a sign she really liked him. But I also remembered his waiting outside my hotel room in New York and the uncomfortable dinner at his mother's condo and Sam picking me up at the orthodontist and waiting for me at my locker and following me down the halls and Sam and Sam and Sam and Sam. . . .

Slowly, he pulled up to the fire hydrant outside

of the Melody Inn. I already had hold of the door handle.

"You're one great guy, Sam. I mean it, and I still like you very much. But I want to be friends and that's all." I looked over at him. "Okay?"

It was not okay. He didn't answer. I waited. Finally he just waved one hand toward the door as if to say, *So go on, why don't you?*

I got out. "Thanks for the ride," I said. And then, "Sam, I'm really sorry," and I closed the door. Running inside, I went straight back to the stockroom, where I sat on a couple of boxes. I was breathing hard.

David—who's a few years older than me—followed me back. "You okay?" he asked.

"Yes," I said. Then, "No. I just broke up with one of the nicest guys in the world."

"Oh?" He came over and sat on a box across from me. "How's that?"

It was as though David was already a priest and I had come to him for confession, and I'm not even Catholic! "Is it possible for someone to be *too* nice, David?" I wondered if anyone had ever said that about *him*.

He studied me. "Nice, as in . . . ?"

"Always there! Always kissing! Always needy! Always wanting me, me, me till I'm almost sick of myself! It's like . . . like he and his mom . . . like he filters everything through her eyes. Like some-one else is pulling the strings. I mean, I don't want a guy who's just excited about *me*; I want him to be excited about *life,* you know? His own life. His own decisions. Am I making any sense at all?"

"Perfectly. But that might be a lot to ask of a guy his age," David said. "Most guys have no clue what they're going to do in life. Look at me. I'm still debating the priesthood. Maybe you're the first thing—the first person—he's ever been excited about. Maybe this is the closest he's got to making life plans."

"Arrggghhh!" I said, clutching my head. "I'm *sixteen*! I don't want to be part of anyone's life plan yet! Sometimes he talks like he's twenty-six!"

Marilyn stuck her head through the curtain in the doorway. "Customers are waiting," she called. And then, "Something wrong?"

"I just broke up with Sam," I told her.

"Oh my gosh!" she said, stepping inside. "Are you okay?"

"Not really," I said. "But I won't be bringing him to your wedding."

"Bring anyone you like," said Marilyn. She came over and put her arm around my shoulder. "Are you *sure* you're okay?"

I nodded. "You don't have to put me on suicide watch or anything," I told her, and managed a weak smile.

All afternoon, though, I relived that conversation in the car. I had no idea I was going to do that. To do it then, anyway. It was so abrupt! I knew how Sam must be feeling. Remembered how I had felt when Patrick and I broke up. I worried that Sam might really be taking this hard. Was that love, being this concerned about him?

What helped, I guess, was that Sam didn't change. When I got home from work that evening, there was a message on my cell phone to call him, but I didn't. On Monday he even sent flowers. If he wasn't trying to please his mom, it seemed, he was trying to please me. All Sam could think of to do were all the things that made me break up with him in the first place.

I had spent all of Sunday on the phone with Liz, with Pamela, with Gwen. I'd started calling them before I went to the "Our Whole Lives" class at church and continued calling when I got home. I wanted to tell them how awful I felt, relieved I felt, guilty I felt, free I felt. . . . Mostly they just listened, which is the very best thing a friend can do.

By Friday Sam had stopped calling and leaving messages. And I was relieved when I saw him around school to know he hadn't thrown himself off a bridge or anything.

It was so weird, really, that the very things girls

talk about wanting guys to do turned me off a little when Sam did them. They hadn't at first. I'd loved all the little considerate things he'd done, and I'd really fallen for him. I thought—and still think—he's one of the nicest guys I've ever met. But sometimes, maybe, when you get to know a person as more than a friend, the chemistry just isn't there. Something gets in the way. You begin to see things you hadn't noticed before, and it's like a big yellow CAUTION sign lighting up inside your head. No matter how much I'd *try* to love him, no matter whether or not I thought I *should*, if I didn't or couldn't, it wasn't fair to stick around. I had to keep reminding myself of that.

And then on Saturday, his mother called. When she told me who she was, I almost dropped the phone.

"Oh, hi," I said, and waited, my heart pounding. Was she going to bawl me out for breaking up with her son?

"This is a belated birthday present, Alice," she said, "but I'd be glad to do a professional portrait of you if you'd like to come over sometime."

I couldn't even answer, so she went on: "I do lots of portrait photography, and I often do things for Sam's friends. It would be my present to you. Just tell me when you'd like to come over, and I can set up the lights and camera right here."

"Oh . . . um . . . thanks," I said. "I don't know . . ."

"Well, think about it," she said, and gave a little laugh. "The offer's good for a month. My treat."

"Thanks," I said again. And then, without waiting for her to say it first, "Good bye." I hung up, and the phone was wet with my perspiration.

Had she actually done that? Called the girl who had dumped her son and tried to bribe her back again with a photo session? Had she done the same with Jennifer? Did Sam know? Had he *asked*?

I made two decisions right then, and one was so mature, I surprised even myself. First, I would not go. Second, I wouldn't tell any of my friends about the phone call. If I did, it would be all over school that Mrs. Mayer had tried to get me back with Sam again, and he was too nice a guy for that.

"Maybe you *are* growing up," I said aloud, looking at myself in the hall mirror.

It was hard to figure out, really—Sam and his mother. Maybe it had to do with the fact that his father wasn't there. Maybe his mom felt Sam was all she had left and was trying to set up his future for him. Maybe Sam was the kind of guy who didn't do well alone, who always had to have a girl in his life. I didn't have to understand him, though. I just had to be honest about what worked for me, and that relationship just never completely jelled, that's all. Pamela had to discover she was more than a body part, Faith had to convince herself she wasn't a doormat, and I had to accept the fact that I wasn't a life preserver. Sam's whole life couldn't depend on me.

Of course, I didn't have anybody waiting in the wings. I'd given up the security of going out with a guy whenever I wanted—his kisses and more. But I felt about a zillion times stronger than when Patrick and I broke up. I was still the same me, and I didn't need a boyfriend to prove it.

But some of my friends just couldn't let it drop.

"So what happened?" Karen asked in the locker room at P.E. "Tell us everything."

"I felt like I was suffocating," I said.

"He *was* getting on our nerves in New York," Elizabeth told them, "but—I don't know—if it had been Ross and me, I think I'd have wanted him around all the time."

"That's probably the way most people feel when they're in love, so I guess I wasn't in love," I said.

"You looked like you were in love at the dance," Jill said, studying me hard. "You looked like you were in love on the bus from New York. *Especially* on that bus!" She gave me a wicked smile.

"I know. But he liked me more than I liked him, and it just didn't seem fair to go on pretending."

This didn't seem reason enough, though, to Jill and Karen, and they kept trying to figure it out. "He wanted to go to third base, and you wouldn't let him?" Karen guessed.

I just laughed. "Maybe if he'd tried, I *would* have let him," I joked. "I liked all that." Maybe that was one of the reasons I'd broken it off, I thought. I'd liked that, but I hadn't liked Sam enough to continue. It wasn't honest. In a way, Pamela had been more honest with Hugh, because when she did what she'd done, she was nuts about him.

The girls were still guessing.

"You're not the same religion. Was that it?" Penny asked.

"We didn't even discuss it."

"His mom?" Karen said, and looked right into my eyes.

I knew that if we got into that, I'd say more than I should. "It was a little bit of everything. When you come right down to it, I just wasn't crazy enough about him, and Sam deserves more than that," I told them.

23

Changes

On Wednesday, Mr. Ellis called an end-of-the-year cast-and-crew meeting. Ever since that fiasco with Hugh in the cafeteria, Pamela had retreated to a daily routine and not much else, afraid, I guess, that if she took one step out of line, she'd run into him somewhere. I dragged her along to the crew meeting just to add some variety to her day.

Molly and Faith and Pamela and I sat down in the second row, waiting for everyone to get there.

"Okay, listen up," Mr. Ellis said when he came in. "I know you're busy, but every year about this time we get requests from the community for performers at various events. The choir gets requests for the madrigal singers, the drama department gets requests for readings or skits. We like to be part of the community, because the community supports our productions, but it's not easy this time of year to find performers. . . ."

Groans from the cast.

"Last year," Mr. Ellis went on, "we sent a few small groups out to sing some numbers from *Fiddler,* but there isn't really any good section from *Father of the Bride* that works well on its own."

"Not to mention that we can't squeeze one more thing into our schedules!" said the senior girl who had played the part of the bride.

"I know that. I'm just fishing for answers here. I've looked up a couple of short pieces I think would work for a meeting of the Rockville Women's Club and one for the Lions' Club of Silver Spring. The Hospital Volunteers want to be entertained too. The piece that would work best, I think, requires a girl and a guy at a dance, each telling the audience what's going on in their heads. Anybody interested in memorizing about two pages and doing these performances?"

"The prom's coming up, Mr. Ellis!" said somebody.

"We've got exams!"

"Count me out," said someone else.

"Please . . . ?" Mr. Ellis pleaded.

"Pamela can do it!" I offered suddenly.

Pamela, who had been sitting slouched down in her chair, suddenly bolted upright. "Alice!"

"Yeah, Pamela Jones!" said Molly.

"She's good!" I went on. "We were in a production together back in sixth grade."

Pamela stared at me wide-eyed. "A production? You were a bramble bush!" Everyone laughed.

Mr. Ellis smiled. "Can you come up here and give it a try, Pamela?" Mr. Ellis said. "It's humorous. I think you'd like it."

"I'll read the guy's part," said Harry, grinning. "C'mon, Pam."

"*Pam*-ela! *Pam*-ela! *Pam*-ela!" Molly and Faith and I chanted, slapping our thighs to the beat.

Harry came over and grabbed Pamela's hand, pulling her up on the low practice stage. Pamela's face was pink, and she looked around uncertainly.

"Okay, here's the situation," Mr. Ellis said, handing both Pamela and Harry a copy of the dialogue. "Boy is watching girl across the room and is trying to get up his nerve to approach her, to ask her to dance. She's doing the same, wanting and yet afraid that he'll come over. You guys take it from there."

Harry began, and he's so expressive, I wondered why he was content to work backstage instead of trying out for a part each year. "There she is," he said to the audience. "Girl of my dreams. I'm within ten feet of her, and already she can tell I'm a quivering mass of jelly."

Pamela cleared her throat and read her lines

next, but her voice was so soft and unsure that we could scarcely hear her. I could tell that Mr. Ellis was disappointed.

"A little louder, Pamela?" he coached.

"I've been . . . watching him . . . all evening and . . . ," Pamela said, still flat and uninspired. My heart sank.

"Pamela," Molly called. "Belt it out, sweetie!"

"You can do it!" said Faith.

"Even a bramble bush could do it!" I teased, and made her laugh.

I saw her glance at Harry again. Then she took another breath, and this time we could hear her all over the room as she exaggerated the lines.

"I've been watching him all evening, and if he walks over here, I will absolutely wilt!" she said.

"Now, that's more like it," said Mr. Ellis. "Go on, Harry."

"I'm going to move my left foot now," Harry continued, taking a step toward Pamela. "My left foot is moving. Now my right foot . . ."

"Oh my God!" said Pamela, sounding exactly like the old Pamela now. "He's moving! He's breathing! He's coming my way!"

And we all clapped and cheered.

"I think I've got my volunteers," said Mr. Ellis.

I could have run up onstage myself and hugged Harry for getting her up there; hugged Mr. Ellis for giving her a chance; hugged Faith and Molly for making her feel useful again.

There was a practice session for them every day after school, and on Friday when Pamela was hurrying off to meet Harry, Brian leered at her, the way he does, and called out, "Hey, hot stuff! What's *with* you, anyway? New personality or something?"

"New direction," Pamela called back without skipping a beat.

Saturday after work when Pam was sitting out on the front porch with me, helping me cram for the written part of my driver's test, we got to talking—I mean, *really* talking—about what had happened with her and Hugh.

"I read so much more into it," Pamela said. "I thought . . . I really *thought,* Alice, that he wanted *me*. He kept saying how much he wanted me, how good I was at it—we even kissed afterward. It's not like it was just wham, bam, and it was over. I asked if he'd ever go out with a sophomore, and he said, 'Why not?' And I read into that a million things that weren't there."

"It's easy to do," I said, slowly pushing my feet against the floor of the porch. The swing moved back and forth, the chain squeaking lightly on the forward motion.

"He was nice to me on the bus coming back too.

But when I think about it, he was probably already beginning to cool off. And then . . . the way he acted at school . . . like he didn't even *know* me, practically. It was . . . God, I just feel so used. Same old story. What's with guys, anyway? Ron . . . Brian . . . Hugh . . ."

"They're just as different as we are, Pamela. For every Ron, there's a Ross, you know. For every Hugh, there's a Harry."

"I suppose so." She was quiet for a while. "I should have been in that class with you."

"What class?"

"'Whole Self' . . . 'Whole Life' . . . the one that sounds like an insurance company."

"I wish you had been too," I said. "One of our topics was 'Healthy Lovemaking.'"

"I'll take hot, not healthy," she joked. "What'd you learn?"

"That it's consensual, safe, nonexploitive, and mutually pleasurable," I said, spoken like a true teacher.

"*Next* time," said Pamela.

"Listen," I said. "I get to bring a guest to Marilyn's wedding. Want to go? It's next Saturday."

"Can't," she said. "Got a date."

Uh-oh, I thought. Not Tony or Brian . . .

"With Mom," Pamela said. "You're not going to believe this, but we're going hiking."

I was so surprised that I let the *Maryland Driver's Handbook* fall right out of my hands.

"Your *mom*? *Hiking*?" I hit the side of my head with one hand. Was I dreaming? "When did *this* happen?"

"Don't get your hopes up that there's any big breakthrough, but . . . well, you asked me if I was *ever* going to forgive her, and I realized that unless I did, nothing was going to change. The only thing left for her to do was get out of my life completely, and I decided I didn't want that."

"Yeah? And . . . ?"

"She's been seeing a therapist, and I guess the therapist suggested a hike or something where we didn't have to just sit and look at each other."

"I'm stunned!" I said.

She smiled. "So am I. But when I realized how miserable she'd been in New York—I mean, having panic attacks and trying to get a prescription refilled—I don't know. In one way I'm glad she was miserable. I wanted her to feel some of what *I've* been feeling for the last two years. But in another way I felt sorry for her. What can I say?"

"I'm glad for you, Pamela. Really!" I said.

"We're going to spend the day walking along the C&O Canal. She's even packing a picnic lunch. And we agreed on one rule: Each of us can say whatever we want for as long as we want without the other interrupting until we're through."

"Sounds good. Have you told your dad?"

"He says he doesn't care what I do as long as I don't bring her home with me."

"Still," I said, "it's a start."

On Sunday, I had my next-to-last session of "Our Whole Lives," titled "Myths and Facts." If Elizabeth had been there, she probably would have fainted dead away at some of the things we talked about, but by now we were pretty comfortable with each other, and topics like masturbation didn't throw us.

"It's a healthy way to release tensions, and it only becomes a problem if you feel guilty about it or you do it to the exclusion of other things," Gayle said. "Some people feel guilty about their sexual fantasies. Just because you fantasize about something doesn't mean you are going to go out and do it. Most of us would never dream of doing many of the things that turn us on, but it's okay to think about them."

Then Bert talked about all the negative and inaccurate things that have been taught about masturbation—that it makes you crazy or that hair will grow on the palms of your hands. *Ho ho,* we laughed. We all knew better than that, didn't we?

He also said that even grown-ups do it. Even married people do it sometimes!

But then . . . Yikes! Bert divided us into two equal groups. The first formed a small circle, and the second formed a second circle inside the first, facing the others, so that each of us was facing a partner.

"Okay," said Gayle, "I'm going to suggest a topic and set a timer. For one minute—that's about thirty seconds each—you are to talk about that topic with the person you're facing, and when the timer goes off, the inner group moves to the right to the next partner and I'll announce a new topic. Ready?"

I felt a drop of sweat trickle down the small of my back. We heard Gayle set the timer, and it began to tick.

"What did your parents tell you about sex?" Gayle asked.

I was facing the girl who had wanted to climb out a window the first day I came to the class, so I was surprised she spoke first.

"Not much," she said. "It wasn't that they didn't want me to know. They just kept shoving books at me. How about you?"

I thought a moment. "My mom died when I was little, so I learned everything from my dad and older brother," I said. "I can't remember them sitting me down and telling me stuff, but they tried to answer everything I asked. My dad did, anyway. . . ."

Ding went the timer.

"Bye," she said.

I moved one step to the right and faced the wrestler. He grinned. Gayle set the timer.

"Can you remember any inaccurate information you got in the past?" she said.

"That's easy," said the wrestler. "One of my buddies said that you couldn't get a girl pregnant if you had sex standing up."

That made me laugh. "I heard that once a girl used a tampon, she wasn't a virgin any longer," I told him. I actually said that. I said that to a *guy*!

"Never heard that one," he said. "But a cousin told me once that a guy had to limit how often he had sex, because he only had so many orgasms in him before his sex life was over."

I'd never heard *that* before, but the timer dinged again, and there I was, facing Lyle, the tall guy who'd had the word *clitoris* on his back that first day.

"Here we go," said Gayle. "Did you ever come across a sexual term you didn't understand?"

"Necrophilia," I said.

"Nymphomania," the tall guy said.

"Yemani wrigglings and Nubian lasciviousness," I told him.

He stared at me. "O'm'God! Somebody else read the unexpurgated edition of *Arabian Nights*!" he said. "Where did you find your copy?"

"A friend brought it to a sleepover," I said. "Where did you find yours?"

He laughed. "A secondhand bookstore. I went in there after school for a month so I could read the whole thing."

I had to remember to tell Elizabeth.

But now Bert was giving each of us a sheet of paper and an envelope.

"I'd like you to take a full fifteen minutes," he said, "and write down what your own values are regarding your sexuality. These are private, to be read only by you. When you're done, seal them in the envelope and put your name on it."

I was glad no one else would read mine because I wasn't entirely sure of my values. Would they be the same two years from now? Five years? When I was twenty-six? Twenty-nine?

I think I'd have to really like a guy to get involved with him sexually. Right now, ideally, it would be nice to have intercourse for the first time when I'm married, but I don't know that I can promise myself that. I'll see when I get to college. But whenever that is, it's got

*to be somebody I love and trust, and
we've got to have a lot more going for
us than just sex. . . .*

The page was almost full when I stopped writing. I folded the paper up and put it in the envelope, just as Bert handed us another paper.

"Now," he said, "write your name at the top and hand it to the person on your right."

We looked at each other quizzically and passed the papers on.

Bert smiled. "We call this our group appreciation letter," he said. "Starting at the bottom, write a short one-or two-sentence positive, but honest, comment about the person whose name is at the top of the page. Then fold the paper up to cover what you've written and pass it on. Once it's gone all the way around the room, Gayle will collect them, and we'll give them out to you next week at our last session."

We began. You could always tell who had your paper because we tended to look at the person we were writing about. I told the wrestler how funny he was, how he livened up the class. I told the girl who'd wanted to climb out the window that I was glad we'd survived the class together. I told the tall guy that he had asked some of the most interesting questions, and I told his girlfriend that she had given me a lot to think about with some of her comments.

What were they writing about me? I wondered. We weren't supposed to give false praise. Had I spoken up enough? Had I really even let them get to know me? When my paper came back with my name at the top, all folded up like a fan, I handed it to Gayle but would have given anything to stick it in my pocket and take it home.

"Next week's your last class?" Liz said in disappointment when I called her later.

"Yep."

"So what did you talk about today?"

"Sexual myths and facts. Masturbation, in particular."

"I could *never* talk about that in front of a guy, Alice!" she declared. But there was only a two-second pause before she asked, "So what did they say about it?"

"That it's healthy and doesn't make you crazy. And I actually met a guy who'd read the unexpurgated edition of the *Arabian Nights*," I said, referring to the book Liz had smuggled out of her parents' bedroom once. She'd read portions of it aloud to Pamela and me.

"How did you *know*?" asked Liz.

"I mentioned Yemani wrigglings and Nubian lasciviousness," I told her.

"You didn't tell him about *me*, did you?" Liz asked.

"Of course not."

"So what else did you learn?"

"That you can still get pregnant if you have sex standing up," I told her.

There was a longer pause this time. "How exactly does *that* work?" Liz asked.

"I haven't the slightest idea. But Aunt Sally told me once that if I ever had a boyfriend over, I should keep both feet on the floor. I'd better tell her to rethink that one," I said.

24

Alice Was Here!

Dad let me drive to the Maryland Motor Vehicle Administration for my driving test. I was so nervous, I was chewing my gum sixty chews per minute.

"Don't rush yourself," Dad said. "Take your time answering the written quiz. Take your time on the road test. The last thing the instructor wants to see is a quick, impulsive driver."

How do you tell yourself not to be nervous? My palms were wet when I picked up my pencil. But I think I did okay. There were only a couple of questions I wasn't sure of. But when I had to go out for the road test, I was so scared that I had to go to the restroom first, and I kept the officer waiting.

I don't need someone sitting beside me in a cop's uniform. Why couldn't they have put someone beside me in a nurse's uniform holding a glass of water and an aspirin bottle? Why couldn't it be a jolly grandmother with a plate of cookies on her lap? Did I really need a policeman watching me make a U-turn?

His voice sounded like a robot's, actually.

"Take it up to the corner and make a right turn," he said.

That meant I had to get over into the right lane, and I looked behind me to be sure there wasn't a car in my blind spot. I forgot to put on my blinker when I changed lanes. He made a mark on his clipboard.

When he asked me a block farther on to stop and back up, I did it by looking in my rearview mirror instead of turning around and looking over my shoulder. Another mark.

By the time we got to parallel parking, I was semi-hysterical inside. I tried to move the car into a space next to the curb, but I freaked out and was afraid I was going to cut it too close. I pulled out again and tried a second time. This time the front end stuck way out into the roadway and my back wheel hit the curb.

"Take it back in," said the policeman.

"In?" I asked.

"Back to the station," he said.

I felt as though there were a cement block in my stomach. I could see Dad peering through the chain-link fence as I pulled the car into the drive-way at the station. I couldn't even look at him. We went inside, and I followed the officer over to the desk.

He took my application and stamped FAILED on it.

"Better luck next time," he said.

I cried all the way home.

"It's the worst parking I ever did!" I wept. "Even when I was first learning, I never did that bad!"

Dad reached over and patted my knee. "At least you know that you can fail the test and the earth won't swallow you up. You'll do better next time."

I didn't think so. And now I had to tell my friends.

"You blew it?" Pamela said when she heard. "Poor Alice!" Pamela, who passed the first time.

"Totally," I said. Pamela had her license, Brian had his, Sam, Justin, Karen, Molly. . . .

Gwen's old enough, but she hasn't even applied for one yet. Too busy with school, she said, to take the driver's ed course. Elizabeth and Patrick and Mark are all younger than I, and Pamela's dad won't let her drive his car even though she could. But we're on the fringe. Everyone else is driving.

"Oh, Alice, I was a slow learner too," Sylvia told me. "It just took me a long time to get the hang of it. I know how you feel."

Nobody knows *exactly* how you feel. I'd pictured myself driving to the Melody Inn sometimes when Sylvia didn't need her car. Pictured myself picking up Liz and Pamela and driving to the mall. Driving over to Lester's with a plate of brownies. It seemed to me right then as though the whole world was divided between those who could drive and those who had to be driven. Why was *I* always on the losing end of things? When the world was divided between those who had perfect teeth and those who didn't, those who had mothers and those who didn't, I was always in the "didn't" camp there too. I was so down, I even started feeling sorry for myself because I didn't have Sam's shoulder to cry on.

Except that, one thing you learn as you grow up is that—surprise!—you're not the center of the universe. I realized that while failing my road test was a tragedy to me, it was hardly a blip on Dad's radar screen. He was far more concerned about hiring a new trombone instructor at work. Sylvia was involved in end-of-the-year tests in her English class, and Lester had just started his master's thesis.

"The title is *what*?" I said, when he told me.

"'In Defense of Partiality and Friendship: A Critique of Utilitarianism and Kantianism,'" said Lester.

"Oh," I said.

Even my closest friends probably didn't spend more than five minutes a day feeling sorry for me. Pamela, of course, was working on a shaky peace with her mom; Liz was depressed because Ross had decided not to go to Camp Overlook again as a counselor; Gwen had applied for a student internship at the National Institutes of Health.

Get a life, I told myself. *Think global warming. Think world peace.*

What I decided was that I would practice parallel parking every chance I got, but I wouldn't even think about going back for a road test until after Marilyn Rawley's wedding. Since she couldn't be my sister-in-law—something I'd always wanted— at least I could be there to support her when she married someone who wasn't my brother.

I wondered how Lester would take it. When Crystal Harkins married—another old girlfriend of his—I was a bridesmaid at her wedding, and Lester wasn't even invited. I'd seen him come in at the back of the church just long enough to hear her take her vows. Now here was another one who got away. This time, though, Les was bringing his new girlfriend with him.

Lester was sitting on our couch checking dates on his Palm Pilot.

"Les," I said, "do you still have feelings for Marilyn?"

He didn't even look up. "Define 'have feelings,'" he said.

"You know perfectly well what I mean. Do you still think about her or even wish that she was marrying you instead of Jack?"

"Jack's a lucky fellow," he said.

"You didn't answer the question."

"As I remember, it wasn't Marilyn who objected to getting married," said Lester. "So why should I be upset that she's not marrying me?"

"I know. Both Crystal and Marilyn were wild about you and would have married you in a heartbeat. I'm only asking if you're sorry now."

"It was the wrong time to even think about marrying," he said, and punched in another date.

I sat down across from him and rested my hands on my stomach. "Isn't it weird, Les, how you can love a person for all the wrong reasons and *not* love a person for all the right ones?"

"Come again?"

"I mean, sometimes people fall in love with some really awful person and other people fall *out* of love with someone who's really nice."

"It happens," said Lester, and concentrated again on the Palm Pilot.

"Wouldn't it be great, Les, if there was a little chime inside you that only you could hear whenever you were with someone who was just right for you, and if you were with someone who would make your life miserable, you'd hear a buzzer instead?"

"You know, Al, I keep getting this little buzzing sound inside my head, sort of behind my eyeballs," Lester said. "Why don't you try going upstairs, and I'll see if it stops?"

On Marilyn's wedding day that Saturday, the music instructors manned the store while the rest of us went to the wedding. I'd invited Liz. It was a beautiful afternoon, and I was glad for Marilyn and glad for Pamela, too. Hiking with her mom in the rain could be a real disaster. It was going to be difficult enough as it was.

Marilyn and Jack were getting married at a nature center near Seven Locks Road in Bethesda. It was a place she and Jack liked to hike, she'd told me. It would be a simple ceremony beneath a sycamore tree in a meadow. Everyone was invited for refreshments afterward at the little house she and Jack were renting in Rockville.

Dad was wearing a suit, and Sylvia was going in a dress and heels. So I decided to wear the dress with the spaghetti straps I'd worn for their wedding and a pair of beige pumps with a small heel. The panty hose I'd worn to the dance, though, had a hole in one toe, I discovered when I pulled them on. I rummaged around in my drawer until I found the pair I'd worn for Crystal's wedding two years ago and pulled them on just as Elizabeth rang the doorbell, and a couple of minutes later we all climbed in Dad's car.

"Perfect day for a wedding," said Dad.

"Almost as beautiful as ours," said Sylvia, and they smiled at each other. In the backseat Liz and I smiled too. Who could have known three years ago, when I'd invited my English teacher to a Messiah Sing-Along without telling Dad, that they would fall in love and marry? That sometimes fairy tales *do* come true?

We took East-West Highway to Bethesda, then drove down Democracy Boulevard, its center strip lined with pear trees, to the little nature center in the woods behind the tennis courts. A handmade sign with a white satin ribbon on it directed us to a wooden footbridge, which guests were crossing, and into the woods, where every so often another white ribbon marked the way. Some people, like us, had dressed up. Some came in jeans, some in cotton dresses, and a few even arrived in tuxedos and bright red sneakers. A riot. It was all so . . . so *Marilyn*. No rules at all about silly things like clothes.

There were backless wooden benches for about fifty people beneath the tree where a park ranger gave lectures in summer. The only decorations were streamers of blue and white ribbons looped around in the lower branches. A woman in a pale blue dress was playing a dulcimer, soft and airy.

We sat down in the third row and waved to Les and Tracy, who were already there. Tracy was wearing a black and white dress, her hair brushed back from her face. Lester, in the same suit he had worn for Dad's wedding, looked so grown up. For the first time, really, I felt I was looking at a grown man who just happened to be my brother. It was the strangest feeling. Every so often it just hits you— that the guy you used to yell at and tease is a man. You know how he looks in his Mickey Mouse shorts and you remember the smell of his socks and sneakers, yet here he is—transformed. I noticed that he and Tracy were holding hands.

Marilyn and Jack were nowhere in sight, so Liz and I looked over the crowd to see who was hot.

"I'll take the guy in the blue shirt and yellow tie," I whispered to Liz.

"What about the guy with the wavy hair?" she said, and we giggled when the guys caught us looking at them and one of them winked at us.

After a while all the guests seemed to be there, and two fiddle players in black pants, white shirts, and red bow ties stood up. They glanced up the hill toward the nature center, then nodded to each other and struck up a stately rendition of "Here Comes the Bride."

We looked around. Jack was coming down a path on one side of the meadow, Marilyn and her father were coming down a path on the other side. They managed to arrive at the tree at about the same time, where a smiling young minister was waiting for them.

Marilyn's shoulder-length brown hair was swept up on her head and fastened with a wreath of blue and white flowers. Her white dress—cotton, of course, as I'd thought it would be—ended at the ankles and had small white flowers embroidered around the scoop neck.

My eyes traveled back and forth between Marilyn and Jack and Lester and Tracy, with detours now and then to Dad and Sylvia. I listened to the music, the poem, the minister's remarks, and the vows, simple and sincere. Finally:

". . . and now, by the power vested in me, I pronounce you, Jack and Marilyn, husband and wife," the young minister said.

Jack pulled Marilyn to him and kissed her lightly on the lips, and on cue, the two fiddle players struck up a lively tune that sent some birds flying straight up out of the tree. As the rest of us clapped, Jack and Marilyn joined hands and, followed by the fiddlers, began dancing their way back up the main path to the parking lot, the guests getting to their feet and following along behind, some of them dancing too.

As I stood up I felt that something was wrong under my dress, and I couldn't figure out what it was. I took a step and realized that the waistband of my panty hose was halfway down my hips, and the crotch was inching its way down toward my knees. They hadn't felt quite right when I'd pulled them on—as though the waistband's elastic had lost its spring—but they were staying up, I'd been in a hurry, and they were the only other pair I'd had. But now . . .

"What's the matter?" Elizabeth asked, turning around.

Dad and Sylvia had already gone up the path behind Jack and Marilyn, but every time I took a step, I felt the panty hose slide down a little farther. Like I was trying to walk with my pants pulled down, which was exactly what I was trying to do.

"Help!" I said. "My panty hose are slipping."

Elizabeth gave an amused shriek. "What?"

"Something's wrong with my panty hose! I think the elastic's stretched, and they're almost down to my knees!" I grabbed hold of her shoulder to steady myself.

The two guys we'd been watching during the ceremony came over, smiling. I think they thought

I'd lost a heel on my shoe or something.

"Problems?" one asked.

Liz and I stared at them and then at each other and started giggling.

"We're okay, really," Liz said. "My friend here just needs to . . . uh . . . go off in the bushes or something."

"Liz!" I said.

"Oh," said the guy in the blue shirt. "I think there's a restroom up in the nature center."

"She can't make it that far," Elizabeth told them.

"It's not that!" I said quickly. "I just have to take something off."

"Well, hey! All riiiiight!" the first guy said.

"Not everything!" Liz said, making it worse.

Liz and I collapsed in laughter, and the guys went on. When they were gone and the other guests were up the hill, I reached under my dress and pulled off the panty hose. I put my shoes back on, then tried to stuff the hose in the beaded purse Sylvia had given me for my birthday, but they wouldn't fit, and I could never wear them again anyway.

"Give them to me," Liz said. She strung them like a banner between the tree branches, the toe of one here, the toe of the other there. The panty part flapped gently in the breeze like a flag.

Liz grinned. "So everyone will know: Alice was here!" she said.

25

On My Way

I don't know how many people showed up at Jack and Marilyn's. Marilyn didn't care and it didn't matter. She and Jack were renting a little two-bedroom house with a big backyard. There was a keg of beer on the patio, a table of cheese and crackers and fruit, and several cakes, which Marilyn had baked herself. Two of her friends moved around the crowd with trays of small sandwiches, and on one side of the yard seven or eight musicians took turns entertaining us.

There were guitars and fiddles and dulcimers. There was an accordion and a recorder and a vocalist who sang old songs from the 1960s, so there was music for people of all ages. When the two fiddlers teamed up with the accordion player for a polka, almost everyone was dancing on the grass, including Liz and me and the two guys we'd seen at the ceremony. Everyone's wedding should be so joy-ful!

"You two related?" the wavy-haired guy asked Liz.

"Just longtime friends," she said.

"So . . . are you friends of the bride or groom?" asked the guy in the blue shirt.

"Marilyn works for my dad," I explained. "How about you?"

"Friends of the groom," he answered. "And Marilyn couldn't be marrying a nicer guy."

Yes, she could, I thought wistfully. *She could be marrying my brother.* But I was happy that she was marrying someone who would be good to her. She had once been so in love with Lester, but now she had eyes only for Jack. Les seemed to feel the same way about Tracy. When Lester introduced Tracy to Marilyn, I didn't see any regret or bitterness in Marilyn's face. She clung to Jack's arm and paraded him about the yard as though she had been looking for him all her life.

Tracy was just as friendly in return. With heels, she was an inch taller than Lester and, all dressed up, looked slightly older. What really captured my attention right then was a couple who had arrived late. The woman had red hair that almost reached her shoulders. She wore it tucked behind her ears, and she reached up now and then to prop it back where it belonged. The most striking thing about her figure was her breast size, which was probably a 38-D. She was holding a little boy, maybe eighteen months old, and her husband was carrying a diaper bag on a strap over his shoulder.

"Elizabeth!" I said suddenly. "That's Crystal and her husband, Peter. I didn't recognize the longer hair!"

"Who?"

"Lester's number two girlfriend, Crystal Harkins. She was insanely jealous of Marilyn, and I don't think I've ever seen the two of them together."

"You think she's here to cause trouble?" Liz asked.

"Not the way they're getting along. Look at them! Like they're old buddies!"

"Of course!" said Liz. "Now that Marilyn didn't land him either, Crystal can afford to be generous." We laughed.

I felt like a camcorder, taking in the scene around me, my head turning slowly this way and that, my eyes the lens, my ears the recorder. Jack and Marilyn moved about the yard together, but I couldn't say the same for Crystal and Peter. As soon as Crystal saw Lester, she handed her little boy to Peter and went over to grab Les by the arm.

"Hi, stranger," she said, smiling up at him.

Les had a beer in one hand and turned to stare at Crystal, maybe not recognizing her for a moment either.

"Well, for . . . Crystal!" he said, taking a step backward. He looked at Peter trailing along behind, then at their little boy. "So this is the kiddo, huh? Hey, Peter, good to see you!" He reached out and shook Peter's hand, despite the fact that Crystal still had hold of that arm. I wondered if she was trying to get Les to kiss her.

"You still in school?" Peter asked.

"Just starting my master's thesis, so we'll see how that goes," Les said.

"Isn't Jeremy a darling?" Crystal said, reaching for the little boy now, who had stretched out his arms toward her. "We had to miss the ceremony because of him, but don't you think he looks like me, Les?"

"He looks like both of you. Has his daddy's eyes," Lester said diplomatically.

At that moment Tracy came back from the refreshment table holding a plate of small sandwiches for Lester and herself. As she moved up between Crystal and Lester, Crystal gave her a quick glance and said, "No, thanks," and started to talk to Les again.

Had that really happened? I wondered, staring. Could Crystal really be so nonobservant? How would Tracy . . . ? How would Lester . . . ?

But Tracy had class. Boy, did she have class!

"Oh, I'm sorry. I brought these for Lester and myself, but I'd be glad to get you something from the refreshment table," she said.

Crystal did a double take and her face flushed. "Oh . . . Oh, no, thanks! I'm fine!" she said.

"Tracy," Lester said quickly, "I'd like you to meet Crystal Carey. Crystal, this is my friend Tracy Freeman."

"Very nice to meet you," said Tracy.

"You too!" Crystal said, and quickly pretended to wipe something off Jeremy's face.

"Wow!" Liz whispered to me. "Now, that was *good*!"

"Terrific, isn't she?" I said. "Come on, let's dance."

We went back out on the grass, twirling and hopping to the polka music—galloping, really—all over the yard. The guy with the wavy hair and the one in the blue shirt had found some girls their own age, but we didn't care. I knew I'd have perspiration stains and would have to have my dress dry-cleaned, but we were having a ball. I only hoped that Pamela could say the same when *her* day was over.

"Well, I can't say it was fun, but—like you said, Alice—it's a start," Pamela told me when I called her that evening.

"It must have been awkward, especially at first," I commented.

"I didn't give it a chance to get awkward. I cut loose with all the stupid things I've done since she walked out on us—things a mother could have helped me with. I mean, I really let her have it."

"Things like . . . ?"

"Dropping out of Drama Club last year, my grades, fighting with Dad, what happened with Hugh . . . I didn't go into details, of course."

"What'd she say?"

"Mostly she just listened."

"Do you think you resolved anything?"

"Who knows? I mean, what's to resolve? How do you take back what you've done? She acted like a slut, running off like that with some guy and . . ."

In the pause that followed, I wondered if Pamela recognized the breathtaking similarity: Mom with boyfriend in Colorado, daughter with boy in New York. I decided not to put it into words myself.

"So she didn't say much at all?" I asked.

"Oh, yeah." Pamela sighed. "She said there was no way she could make up for running out on us, that she'd really thought when she did it that I'd come live with her and her boyfriend. Well, I tried that, of course, and it was a disaster."

Another pause. Then Pamela's voice grew a little softer. "She said that all she can do now is try to be the best mom she can, but I have to give her a chance—that she's having a pretty hard time of it herself. I mean, I know she's on pills and everything. So I said, yes, I'd give her a chance. Anyway, the lunch she brought was good." Pamela gave a feeble laugh.

More silence.

"There's one thing, though," I told her. "Having a mom doesn't save you from all the stuff that's going to happen to you. I still would have fallen down the stairs at school last year and wet my pants. I still felt weird around Sam's mother. And now that I've got a mom, I'm still having trouble with algebra. It's not like everything would be perfect if your mom were living with you."

"That's what she said too."

"Remember how mad Liz was at her mother because she hadn't known Liz was being molested by a family friend when she was little? I mean, a mom can't help you with something unless you *tell* her about it, right?"

"Well, we agreed to spend one day a month together just doing something where we can talk while we're at it. Mom wanted once a week, but I don't think I'm ready for that much closeness yet."

"It might work," I said.

"Yeah, we made a mental note of how far we

walked along the canal and decided maybe we'd start at that point next time and do another section. See how far we can go. Do you suppose if we walk the whole length, maybe by then we'll be buddies again?"

"I sort of think so," I told her.

The last session of "Our Whole Lives" was what Bert called "Catch-Up Sunday" and Gayle called "Anything Goes." It was a chance to ask any question we still hadn't asked, discuss any topic we'd overlooked, and talk about where we were headed that summer. A lot of the seniors told where they were going to college.

It's funny the way really important questions come out when you know it's your last chance to ask them. The wrestler confided that he still wasn't sure of his sexual orientation—that maybe he'd taken the course a second time to help him figure out whether or not he was gay. And I think—I hope—we all let him know that either way made no difference to us. There was a question about AIDS, another about pornography, and a lively discussion about messages we get from advertising, whether they're directed more to guys or to girls.

I got up the nerve to ask if a man can tell if a woman's a virgin when they have intercourse. Bert said that sometimes it's obvious, because the man will have a hard time penetrating and the woman bleeds. But in other women the hymen doesn't cover much of the opening or it stretches, so there's almost no difference between her and a nonvirgin. Then Gayle told us how in some cultures a bride-to-be is so worried her husband will find out she's had sex before that she pays a lot of money to have a sheep's membrane surgically stitched over her vaginal opening. We all groaned in disbelief. I don't know when I was so glad that I live in the country I do, have the family I do, and go to the church that I do, even though I don't go very often.

Then it was checkout time, and after that, as we all said good-bye and gave Bert and Gayle a hug, they handed each of us our envelope and our group appreciation letter, tied together with blue ribbon, like a diploma.

When I got outside, I saw that Dad and Sylvia were still in the church lounge having coffee after the service. So I sat down on a bench near the front garden and untied the blue ribbon. Then I unfolded the paper with my name at the top and was surprised at how nervous I felt to see what the other kids thought of me—kids a year or two older.

Did anyone ever tell you that your best feature is your smile? Suzanne

You didn't say a lot in class, but whenever you did, it was something worth hearing. Gary

There were comments about my candidness when I talked about myself and the way I never put anyone down. Someone even wrote that she liked my hair.

The last comment was from the red-haired senior, the girlfriend of Lyle, the tall guy. She was probably the prettiest girl there, and just as I'd admired beautiful Miss Cole back in sixth grade, I felt this girl had everything, including a boyfriend and a scholarship to Brown. So I was surprised when I got to her comment at the bottom of the page:

You really listen to other people, Alice. I feel I could tell you anything. Of all the people in this class, you're the one I'd most like to know better. Sonya

What a great way to end the course that I never wanted to take but that I wouldn't have missed for the world.

The euphoria didn't last. I failed my second road test, even though I'd practiced parallel parking almost every day since the last test. *Nobody* fails two times. *Nobody!* When Dad and I got home, I went straight up to my room and shut the door. Real mature.

I hadn't gotten the same man either. This time it was a woman, and she made marks all over the paper. What I didn't discover until later was that she was checking off things I did *right,* but I thought all those marks were against me. I figured I had failed even before we got to parallel parking, and when I made a mess of that too, I just turned off the engine and said, "I can't do this." She changed places with me in the driver's seat and drove me back to the station.

I didn't cry the whole way home—just stared stonily out the window. How could I want something so bad and not be able to do it?

I had to tell everyone at lunch the next day, though, because they asked. The last day of school, and this was how I'd end my sophomore year. The humiliating part was that my chin wobbled and I could feel tears gathering in my eyes. That's the worst. When you bawl in front of friends. I should have cried at home and let it out.

But they were really nice about it.

"I've got my car today," said Molly. "You want to practice in it after school?"

"Pamela and I can help too," said Liz.

Brian said, "You can practice parking behind my Buick, but if you scratch it, I'll sue."

So when classes were out and most of the cars had left the parking lot, I climbed in the driver's seat of Molly's old Ford. Molly rode beside me, Brian took his station near his car, and Liz and Pamela stood like cheerleaders along the curb. Sam came out to get in his own car, and when he saw our practice session, he waved and smiled at me and I smiled back. I'd heard that he'd taken a girl in his Spanish class to the movies, and now they were inseparable at school. I guess girls aren't the only ones who can fall in love with love sometimes.

"Good luck!" Sam called.

I silently wished Sam good luck too. I wished my friends good luck. I wished good luck to the school and the state and the whole wide world, if only I could just pass my driver's test.

As I began to back into the space Brian showed me with his hands how much clearance I had when I began to turn the front wheels. Back and forth I went, again and again. Out and in. Out and in. I wasn't sure how much of this was helpful because Molly's car is wider than Dad's. But my buddies wouldn't give up on me.

Finally, after I'd done it successfully five or six times with Molly in the car, she got out and stood on the side and made me do it alone. They made me circle the parking lot, then come back and pull up close beside the Buick. And then, inch by inch, I turned the wheel and backed Molly's car in the space behind. This time I didn't even scrape the curb with my back wheels, and everyone cheered.

Getting my license had become an obsession with me, and I think that's what did it. I was getting sick of myself. Of worrying about myself. Worrying about that test. Worrying about what my friends would think of me and what friends of friends would think. I wanted to concentrate on something different this summer. *Do* something different. I wanted to tackle something new and plan for something else and go to places I'd never been and meet new people. I wanted to concentrate on other things besides my hair, my clothes, my nails, my periods, my braces, my acne, my weight, my height, my love life or lack thereof. . . . A car would help.

The last week of June, I called Les.

"Holy Moses!" he said. "You don't have that license yet?"

"I just have the road test left to do, Lester."

"Where's Dad?"

"He works late tonight."

"Where's Sylvia?"

"Parent conferences."

"How do I know you're not going to bang up my car?"

"Life is full of risks," I told him, and heard him sigh.

"Okay, I'll come over. When does the MVA close?" he asked.

"We've got an hour and a half," I said.

As we headed out to the MVA in Gaithersburg, Lester driving, he said, "What you need to remember is—"

"I'm going to pass this time, Les. You don't need to tell me anything," I said.

"Just don't let them rattle you."

"I'm going to pass, I'm going to pass, I'm going to pass . . . ," I said.

It was the first man again. This time I took a good look at his uniform, but it wasn't a policeman's—just MVA. He wasn't a nurse or a grandmother with cookies in her lap, though, and I could have used some cookies. If he recognized me, he didn't mention it.

"Take her up to the corner and make a right turn," he said.

I put on my blinkers when I changed lanes and left them on while I made turns. Same drill. Take it down the block, then stop and back up, and this time I made sure to check the rearview mirror *and* look over my shoulder.

When we got to the row of parked cars where I'd been tested before, he had me drive right by, and I began to hope he was going to forget parallel parking. He did. But then he remembered and had me go back. These were obviously the very same parked cars that were there before. Old banged-up cars that were destined to sit there forever, waiting to be bumped again. Somehow the empty spot where I was supposed to pull in looked even smaller. I swallowed.

"Okay. Pull right up there by that car ahead and take her in," the man said.

I pulled up close to the gray car, closer than I had the first time. I was out of my mind, I told myself. I wasn't in Dad's car! I wasn't even in Molly's! This was Lester's, and I'd never practiced in that at all. I think I would have paid anything to have Brian standing out there showing me just how much clearance I had. Inch by inch, I got it in, so close to the curb that I astounded myself. I did it! I was in!

"Good!" the man said. He actually said "Good!" But *then* he said, "Okay, pull her out and drive back to the station."

I had to take it back out again? The space was too small. I was in too far! I didn't think I could possibly pull out again without hitting the car in front of me.

If you got it in, you can get it out, I seemed to hear someone saying to me, and I realized that was what Pamela had said when I was trying to use a tampon for the first time. I smiled and the man looked at me sideways. I quickly turned serious and put the car in reverse again. And inch by inch, inch by inch, I got the car back out and drove us back to the station.

I grabbed hold of Lester and spun him around when my application was approved. "I did it, Les! I did it!" I squealed.

"Hey, hold it down," Les said, glancing around us. "What do we do now?"

I had to get in line to get my picture taken, then wait until my license was processed.

But finally, *finally,* I had in my hand that precious laminated card. In my photo my eyes looked half crazed with delight, but I'd done it.

We went back out to the car, and Lester said I could drive. Out on the road! I couldn't believe it.

"Who's on duty tonight?" I asked him, because either Les or one of his roommates has to be home in the evenings for old Mr. Watts.

"George is on tonight," said Les. "I was planning to take Tracy out, but she has to study. What's in the fridge at home?"

"Nothing good," I said. "Which is why I'm taking you to dinner. Anywhere you want to go."

"Hmmm!" said Lester. "Well, there's a French restaurant that has an excellent filet mignon with béarnaise sauce; a seafood place with whole lobster in drawn butter. Or I could go for rack of lamb or veal scaloppini. . . ."

"Uh . . . Lester . . . ," I said, mentally trying to count the dollar bills in my purse and stay on the road at the same time.

"Or," said Lester, "I'd settle for a crab cake sandwich at the Silver Diner."

"You've got it!" I said, and my grin seemed to take over my whole body. Even my ears were grinning. "I'm on my way."